GABRIELLE LANDI

Paperback Cover by MoorBooks
Dust Jacket by GetCovers
Art by Katherine Macdonald
Case Laminate Art by Jenelle Hovde
Map by Cartographybird
Editing by Lisa Henson

CONTENTS

TO THE UNCHARTED NORTH
THE NORTHLANDS
RIYEL
GALAMERE
THE GREAT NATION OF
GALAMERE
AND
SURROUNDING LAND

ELARU
DELTHU
TO THE SOUTHERN NATIONS

Chapter One
Roan

Running his father's tavern had never been easy, but tripping over his dog every other minute certainly didn't make it easier.

Roan Alder clutched the ledger to his chest with one hand as he reached out to save himself from landing on his face, his fingers barely catching on the edge of his desk. He glared down at Beastie, who looked up at him with her long brown tail wagging.

"You're trouble, you know that?" he grumbled as he sat down at his desk.

Almost as much trouble as these numbers.

Roan scowled at the numbers in the ledger in front of him. He had thought that as he grew more experienced, he would find it easier to turn a profit, but things were still getting worse.

Poring over the accounts would only make him crankier.

He slammed the ledger shut, getting to his feet and heading out the door of his office. Beastie jumped to her feet and followed him, her long tail wagging and thumping against his thigh as she passed him in the doorway. He closed and locked his office door behind him as he made his way to the front room, where his patrons gathered, toasting each other after another long day.

Normally, he would have enjoyed the levity, but not tonight. He'd been put off by the increasingly gloomy forecast for this year's profit—or, should he say, lack of profit.

The door opened to let in one of his regulars, who entered to cheers from the men who knew him. It was still light outside, though most of the curtains were drawn and the tavern lit by lanterns, because his patrons spent more of their coins when it felt later than it truly was. Even if most of them hadn't eaten their evening meal yet—they'd be waiting for Abigail to announce that it was ready—they would be more free with their funds in a dim room.

But thanks to the unwanted invoice, Abigail was behind the bar instead of in the kitchen. She slid a mug of ale down to Conrad, who nodded at her in gratitude before taking a swig.

Roan liked Conrad. He was one of the few who came and enjoyed a drink but didn't over-enjoy himself.

Unlike two other men sitting across the room, having a grand old time, laughing raucously and toasting each other with glee.

Roan scowled.

Abigail should have cut them off already.

The baker had brought his weekly bill, so Roan had stepped out to put it into the ledger. He shouldn't have let himself get distracted by the numbers and how they didn't add up—now those two were taking advantage of his absence.

He had zero tolerance for men taking advantage of the fact that his barmaid was relatively new and inexperienced. He might be known across town for being rough, but Abigail was under his protection, and he took that seriously.

He chirped for Beastie and stalked across the room, crossing his arms as he arrived at the table, Beastie by his side.

"Gentlemen," he said sternly, "is there a problem here?"

Silas had the decency to look ashamed, but Gerald Montgomery didn't care. "You can't blame us for having a drink when the whole point of your establishment is drinking," he said, his words beginning to slur.

It was far too early in the night for this.

Roan's stomach turned. "You know I don't tolerate drunks," he said. "You're done for the night, Montgomery. Both of you."

The man grumbled, but before he could say anything, Beastie let out a yip. Montgomery turned white and closed his mouth. He'd run afoul of Beastie one time, and there had been very little trouble with him since.

Roan had more reasons than that to dislike Montgomery—he'd led Roan to believe that his daughter wanted Roan's advances, when she'd wanted nothing more than to run away from him.

If the man didn't spend so much money at the Lucky Goat, he'd be banned.

"Relax," Montgomery muttered, anxiously looking toward the door. "This is my last one."

"Yes, it is," Roan said curtly.

The man drained the rest of his drink before slamming the mug down on the table.

"Be careful," Roan barked. "That's my grandfather's mug. You'd better not let me catch you abusing it again."

It was one of the few things he had left of his grandfather.

"Maybe you won't catch me coming back," Montgomery snarled as he stumbled toward the door, Silas following a moment later.

If only that were true.

Roan watched them leave, a wave of heat flooding his neck as he made his way back to the bar, where Abigail looked up at him with sympathy in her blue eyes.

He didn't want sympathy.

"I can take care of this," she offered, "if you need to take the rest of the night off—"

"I don't need the night off," he said roughly. "I'm fine. Next time, cut them off."

"Of course," Abigail said with a cheerful smile. "I wasn't going to give them any more," she added, "and I'm glad you and Beastie were able to make that clear so I didn't have to."

Her cheerfulness was annoying.

"See that you do," he said, ignoring the rest of what she'd said to focus on the fact that she'd planned to cut them off. "I won't have drunks here."

"I'm aware," Abigail said with a smile. "I won't let that happen. You have my word."

He eyed her sideways as he walked around the bar and reached for one of the mugs she'd been cleaning.

She always did a perfectly fine job, so there was no need for him to inspect it, but it gave him something to do while he gathered his thoughts and pretended he knew what to do with her and the way she was never rattled by anything.

When he glanced back in her direction, she was watching him with a slight smile playing on her lips. "I'm going to pop back into the kitchen, if that's okay. I need to stir the stew."

Roan nodded, and she disappeared around the back before he could say anything else, her blonde curls bouncing as she walked.

She even walked with pep in her step.

This was the problem with hiring her. Roan didn't have a problem with women; he had a problem with people who were too cheerful and wouldn't be grumpy with him.

He never should have hired her in the first place.

"She had it handled," Conrad said from his seat across the bar.

"Sure she did," Roan said gruffly.

"You don't have to be so hard on her," Conrad pointed out.

"I'm not hard on her," Roan said. "I'm simply telling her what needs to be done."

Conrad raised his eyebrows. "You think that's what you're doing?" he asked. "Because from my end, it looks like you're being hard on her."

"It's not your business how I manage my employee," Roan said sharply.

Conrad shrugged his shoulders. He was also far too unruffled—maybe Roan didn't like him either.

"If that's what you say," Conrad said quietly, "though I still think she puts up with more from you than she ought to."

"I'm her employer," Roan said again, but Conrad simply smiled, shrugged, and turned away, going back to nursing his ale.

The door was thrown open with a bang, and Roan looked up quickly. Who was abusing his grandfather's door like that?

The man who stood in the doorway was unfamiliar—short, with blond hair in a terrible cut and ill-fitting clothes. His cloak was torn in the front and showed signs of being mended more than once. Roan frowned. Honest men could be down on their luck, but there was something shifty about this one.

The heavy wooden door slammed shut, and Roan gritted his teeth. He kept the hinges well oiled; there was no need to slam the door to shut it.

The man's hand came around from behind the folds of his cloak, a white rose grasped in his fingers, and Roan saw red.

That was it.

He stalked around the corner of the bar, Beastie immediately following him.

"Why do you have one of my grandmother's roses?" he asked as he approached the stranger, his voice harsh and unforgiving. "No one is allowed to touch those."

"Perhaps you should make a sign," the man said, his voice haughty. "How is one to know that they shouldn't touch your precious roses if there's nothing to tell them that? They're not that pretty, anyway." He threw the flower to the ground.

Roan's hands curled into fists unbidden. Who was this stranger to come and cause trouble at The Lucky Goat? His grandparents had built this tavern with their blood, sweat, and tears, and this man had no respect for any of it. First, he'd thrown the door open so hard Roan had thought it might crack, and now he was insulting his grandmother's roses.

“You are not welcome here,” he said. Perhaps it was hasty to throw out a potential paying customer, but it didn’t seem as if he could pay anyway, and Roan wasn’t here to be a charity.

If the man wanted charity, he should go see his brother Nathaniel, who seemed far more focused on doing good than maintaining what had been left to them by their grandparents.

“I think you should be careful,” the man said, returning his hand to his pocket, his other hand moving to his cloak pocket.

Roan tensed and clicked his tongue for Beastie, who waited by his side, ready for what was to come. If there was to be a knife fight, he wouldn’t want Beastie to be wounded, but the dog was often better than he was at stopping fights before they began.

“You should leave,” Roan said, making an effort to keep his voice more measured. If the man was ready to start a fight, he needed to calm down. He needed to keep his head straight if he was going to be defending himself.

It was his duty to protect everyone in this tavern—not to mention himself.

“Now, now,” the man said, clicking his tongue. Roan reached down to put his hand on Beastie’s head, ready to unleash her if necessary. "I think that this is all a little hasty. After all, I was told to come visit your establishment, but I suppose that you may not be as welcoming as I was led to believe. Perhaps I should make you a little more welcoming."

What did that mean?

The man continued, mumbling to himself. "Perhaps you should learn to think more of the people in front of you than the roses."

Roan took a step forward, Beastie staying right at his side.

"I think you'd better leave, sir," he said, his gaze shifting between the man's face and his hidden pocket.

"Yes, I think that's it," the man said. As he pulled his arm out of his pocket, Roan braced himself to lunge. He stopped short as he noticed it was not a knife, but merely a stick with a small brown egg on the bottom of it.

He barked a laugh. The man had come to threaten him with a stick?

"You should be less of a beast," the man said, acid dripping from his voice as he waved the stick toward Roan. "Until you learn to care more for people, may you never wake again."

He looked down at the stick with a puzzled grimace, banging it on the heel of his other hand. “Already out of power?” he said, groaning. “How?”

Roan had seen enough—the man was clearly mad.

He stepped forward to reach for him and take him to the sheriff when the man pointed the stick again with a triumphant “ha,” and a burst of light came out of it, striking Roan squarely in the chest.

Roan startled, but it didn’t hurt.

It hadn’t done anything.

The man turned and ran, and Roan chased after him, reaching out to snag his arm as the man crossed the threshold. But as his body reached the doorstep, he hit something, and his tavern faded into a sparkling rose-colored void.

Chapter Two
Abigail

Abigail stirred the stew as the scent of fresh bread filled the air, and she smiled in satisfaction at the three loaves she had just taken out of the oven.

Experimenting with baking their own bread instead of buying from the baker every day had been her idea, and this new recipe smelled successful. She'd have to wait a moment if she wanted to see what they truly looked like on the inside without the crumb being damaged by her trying to slice them before they cooled...but she was far too impatient.

She reached for a knife and used a clean towel to pick up one of the loaves. Perhaps cutting one of them wouldn't hurt. It wasn't as if she would use all three loaves of bread tonight, anyway.

She sliced off the heel, releasing even more of that delicious scent into the air, and her stomach grumbled. She usually ate with Roan after they closed up, and she had already eaten a meal before the evening rush began, but surely she could enjoy one slice of bread without too much chaos unfolding in the tavern.

Reaching for the butter crock in the corner, she spread a generous portion on the bread before taking a bite. She closed her eyes and hummed in satisfaction as she chewed. It was perfect. Her father may not have taught her much, but he had certainly taught her how to make a good loaf of bread. Adapting the recipe to the amount of bread the tavern required instead of two people had been a challenge, but she'd figured it out.

Having stirred her stew and tried her bread, Abigail took a deep breath and prepared to head back out to the bar. It had been a busy evening, and after Roan had tucked himself away with the baker's invoice in his office, the men had gotten a little more rowdy.

Nothing she couldn't handle, of course, and if she had asked, Roan would probably have left Beastie with her,

But she wanted to prove to him that she could do it, even if she felt slightly out of her element. She liked this job better than being the washerwoman at the inn she was living at, and if she was going to keep it, she needed to be able to handle herself amongst even the roughest crowds.

She knew she could. She had grown up with worse...so she knew how to handle it, even if she'd rather not.

Now that Roan had cut off Silas and Montgomery and they were gone, perhaps things would get easier—or at least the men would settle down a little, even if the night remained busy.

The spicy-sweet smell of a dragon power-infused magic flooded her senses, and Abigail froze. A blast of rosy light showed through the crack in the kitchen door before everything faded to black for a moment.

Abigail opened her eyes and the light returned, a whisper of the sparkling wind that usually accompanied a curse brushing through her hair.

Who was using magic here, in the Lucky Goat? Magic was illegal in Galamere, and anyone who knew how to use magic would never dare to do so in public—much less inside a tavern full of men.

Though perhaps that was why they felt safe enough to do it. Magic could easily be explained as the drunk ravings of a man who'd had too much.

She forced herself to take a deep breath.

No one knew she knew about magic. No one here, anyway. And if she wasn't out there while they put to rights whatever had happened...she could pretend she didn't know anything about it.

Except Roan might need her help.

She hurried to the door, opening it and surveying the room.

There was no one there.

Well, no one she didn't recognize, that is—only the front door swinging closed behind a dark cloak, with Roan giving chase.

"What happened?" Abigail asked, glancing around the room at the men sitting there. But before they could answer, their heads began nodding to the side, their eyes closing, and those sitting at the bar slumped over, their heads collapsing to the table.

Abigail's eyes widened in alarm, and she rushed forward to catch Conrad as he began to slip off his stool.

"Steady," she said, but he was too heavy for her to hold up, so she could only support him as he fell to the floor, holding his head to prevent him from cracking it.

What sort of magic was this? She hadn't been affected...but this was more than a standard sleeping spell for everyone in the tavern to fall asleep so quickly.

Her stomach churned. Why was she not affected, and where had Roan gone?

There was a yip, and Abigail turned to see Beastie standing over Roan, who was laid out flat on the floor.

Oh. There he was.

Was she the only one awake?

"What happened, Beastie?" Abigail asked as she hurried over.

If only the dog could tell her what was wrong, or what had happened since she stepped into the kitchen.

This was clearly the work of a strong magic user—or someone who had access to a dragon egg.

The thought made bile rise up in her throat. Why would someone with access to a dragon egg be using it against Roan and the tavern? What else were they doing? And how long before they brought attention to the Northlands for illegal magic use?

Before she could continue to think about all the ways everything could go wrong, Roan stirred with a groan. "Roan," she exclaimed, leaning over him. Was he going to wake up?

Her hair fell over her shoulders and into his face, the blonde a strong contrast to his brown beard and short hair, and she immediately backed up—she hadn't meant to be that close to him. His nose twitched as her hair tickled him, and he opened his eyes, confusion filling them. This close, the dark brown she'd always thought they were appeared more hazel. "What happened?" he asked, struggling to sit up.

Abigail scrambled to get away from being uncomfortably close to him before offering a hand to help him sit.

He waved her away, using Beastie to help himself up instead, his gaze unfocused as he stared at the door. "I almost had him," he said suddenly, turning to her just as fast, wincing at the movement. ""Where did he go?"

"Where did who go?" Abigail asked. "I didn't see what happened."

"There was a troublemaker," he said, growling again. Did he realize how scary his voice was when he did that? "Where did he go?"

"I didn't see him," Abigail responded patiently. He'd already asked that. Had he hit his head when he landed?

"I need to sit down," Roan said, reaching out and putting his hand on her shoulder.

That was new. Abigail wasn't sure if he had ever touched her before.

"You are sitting down," she pointed out.

Roan looked down at his feet with a glare. "What did he do to me?" he asked.

"I'm not sure," Abigail replied quietly, "but you're not the only one."

Roan's head turned around so fast he might have given himself whiplash, and when he saw the tavern full of sleeping men, he swore under his breath.

"I'm going to find him and make him undo it," he said, staggering to his feet with Beastie's help.

"The thing is, I don't know how you'll find him," Abigail said, getting up and reaching for his arm. He shook her off but then faltered, and when she reached for his arm again, he allowed her to take it and offer him support.

"I don't like it," he growled again.

"I don't, either," Abigail pointed out evenly, "but perhaps it would be best for you to sit down for a moment before we try to figure out where he went."

"I don't want to sit down," Roan grumbled.

Abigail nearly rolled her eyes.

Of course, he didn't want to sit down. He never wanted to sit down in the front room, but in this case, he didn't have much choice.

She helped him to the closest empty booth, Beastie sticking to his side, ignoring all the men sleeping in the rest of the tavern.

This was certainly more than she had expected to deal with today, but her upbringing had prepared her for this.

Maybe.

She could help somehow...but how, she wasn't sure.

She'd never really discovered where her talents lay, and without a dragon egg to draw power from, she didn't know that she would be powerful enough to attempt to undo whatever spell this was—not that she knew how to do that, even if she did have a dragon egg.

She sighed and slumped onto the seat across from Roan, who was staring at the table, his eyes unfocused even as his hands ran through Beastie's fur. Abigail turned her attention to him.

"Does your head hurt?" she asked quietly.

"Of course my head hurts," he snapped. "I ran into something when I was trying to catch him."

That didn't sound good.

"You ran into the door?" Abigail asked.

"No," Roan said shortly. "It was before the door. I don't know what happened."

Abigail thought she might know—and it wasn't a good sign.

But whether there had been a spell placed to keep them in the tavern or not, the fact that this many men had been put to sleep and were still asleep didn't bode well.

Whoever had cast this was playing with a powerful magic and had far greater power than she did.

"We'll figure it out," she said.

"I don't need your help." Roan's words were gruff, and she resisted the urge to roll her eyes.

"Of course, you need my help," she said. "We're in the tavern with everyone around us asleep. Surely, you don't think it's a coincidence that I'm still awake."

Roan muttered something under his breath, and Abigail sighed. He wasn't going to make this easy.

"Whether we like it or not, we're going to need each other's help to figure this out."

He did not seem amused. "We shouldn't be in this position," he muttered.

"And yet we are," Abigail said with forced cheerfulness. "So we'll have to make the best of it."

"How exactly do you suggest making the best of this?" Roan asked, gesturing to the men sleeping around them. "Should we throw a party while my business goes under?"

"You're not going to go under," Abigail said, as patiently as she could. "But we should try to figure out what's going on here, so we can decide what we're going to do next."

Roan grunted and staggered to his feet. "Gonna go find him. Make him make it stop," he said. His steps faltered as he made his way toward the door with Beastie beside him.

"Roan, be careful," she called out, the words barely leaving her mouth before Roan bounced backwards. Somehow only his head landed on Beastie, who yelped.

Abigail sighed.

"What is that?" Roan asked, sitting up and turning to her with a glare.

As if any of this was her fault. "It looks like we're stuck here," she said as cheerfully as she could. "We'll have to figure out what we're going to do now, without being able to leave. Do you remember if he said anything before he left?"

Roan shook his head, carefully rubbing the side of it. "I don't remember," he said, panic lacing his voice. "I don't remember anything."

Beastie leaned up against his side as if to lend him comfort, and his hand moved to rest on her honey-colored head.

He'd never been the most pleasant man, but seeing him reduced to this was nothing she would ever wish upon a man. "It's okay," Abigail said in the same way she might soothe a panicked child, letting warmth infuse her voice. "We'll figure it out. You're not alone."

Roan glared at her. "I'm an adult," he said. "I don't need to be coddled."

"I know you don't," she said in a rush, "but you just hit your head and it's okay if you don't remember things, I'm sure it'll come back to you eventually, and even if it doesn't, that's okay, we'll figure it out and—"

"You're talking too much," he said, interrupting her nervous stream of thought. "My head hurts."

Abigail sighed.

Hitting his head hadn't changed him, apparently.

He looked around the tavern, and she could hear the mostly hidden fear in his voice as he said, "What if they never wake up?"

"They will," Abigail said, her voice carrying a confidence she didn't feel. "I know they will."

Roan gave her a sideways glance before getting to his feet and stomping away. Beastie looked between her and Roan as if she wasn't sure whether to stay with Abigail or go with her master.

"Go with him," Abigail said to Beastie, nodding in the direction of his office. "He needs you."

Beastie promptly followed Roan, and Abigail sighed, planting her hands on her hips as she surveyed the tavern. There was no way of knowing how long it would take to break this curse, especially if Roan couldn't remember the conditions of it.

Most curses had a failsafe woven into them, and it was only a matter of time until they figured out what this one's was, but until then, things might get sparse.

While there was no way of knowing how long it would take them to break this particular curse, she had heard of curses that lasted years. And if they couldn't leave the tavern, she and Roan would have to become self-sufficient.

She made her way to the kitchen and reached for the back door carefully. She didn't want to bounce off a barrier the way Roan had. But as she carefully opened the door, she was delighted to find that she was able to step through it into the back garden.

While they hadn't used it for much, it wouldn't be hard for her to plant a couple more things, in case the curse lasted longer than she wanted.

Not that there was too much time left in the short growing season of the Northlands...but anything would be better than nothing.

Abigail took a deep breath of the fresh air and turned to enter the tavern in search of seeds, but stopped when a ball was thrown over the back fence.

She made her way over to throw it back, picking it up and hefting it in her hands.

It looked familiar.

Too familiar.

It looked exactly like the homemade ball made of fabric scraps that had been thrown over the back wall a few days ago. She remembered it because Beastie had brought it to her, shredded into many pieces.

But how could that be?

The only way the same ball could have appeared was if whoever had cast the spell was dabbling in much stronger magic than they ought to, and an involuntary shiver raced down her spine at the thought.

Surely they hadn't been sent back in time. Was that even possible without using dark magic?

But it fit with everything else she knew about this curse.

Abigail left the ball where it was. Beastie would find it later and destroy it just as she had the first time, and hopefully Roan would remember what had happened before the time ran out on this curse.

She didn't want to think what it meant if he didn't.

Chapter Three
Roan

Roan paced back and forth in his office, struggling to remember anything past the moment when the man had pointed the wand at him. He hadn't thought magic was real until today, but now it was plain to see.

Not only was it real, it was dangerous.

What had happened, and how was he going to break the curse that held him trapped in his tavern?

What was he going to do if the doors never opened again?

Would he and Abigail die of starvation?

What would happen to the sleeping men in the tavern? Would they wither away in front of him? Would he be forced to watch as the few people he knew and liked, the few people who didn't hate him, remained forever trapped in a sleeping curse?

He fought the urge to retch as Beastie flopped into the corner and watched him silently, no longer putting in the effort to try to keep up with him.

Would she be able to go into the back garden, or would he end up with a pile of dog excrement in the corner of his office?

He should have checked if they could get into the garden or not. Maybe he could scale the fence and get out that way.

Or maybe this was all a bad dream, and he would wake up soon.

That made much more sense than a ruffian with a magical stick attacking him in his own tavern.

Perhaps that was the answer, and this would all disappear shortly. Yes, that had to be it.

It was only a dream.

Roan reached for the bottom drawer of his desk and pulled out a hammer. If he was dreaming, he might as well get the enjoyment of accomplishing a few things from his never-ending list of things to do, like fixing the booth that was separating from the wall.

He made his way out of his office, walking past a surprised Abigail, who glanced down at the hammer in his hands.

"Gonna fix that booth," he said, gesturing with the hammer.

She raised an eyebrow at him, seemingly surprised by his decision to accomplish something. He shrugged. "Might as well make something happen while I'm dreaming."

Not that he owed her an explanation. She should know better than to expect one from him, but she'd been helpful when he'd been stuck on the floor, so perhaps he should at least clue her in on the fact that they were stuck in a dream together.

Or maybe she wasn't even aware of it. Maybe it was simply his dream, and she was only a character in the story.

It didn't matter.

He was going to fix the booth to pass the time until he awoke.

He made his way over and used the hammer to pull out the nails that had started to slide out of the wall. He carefully pounded them straight again and put them in a new spot before hammering them through the back of the booth into the wall.

This was satisfying, at least.

He tried not to glance over at all the men sleeping around him, because when he did, he had the feeling that this might not be a dream after all—and that was far too unsettling an idea for him to entertain for long.

But they hadn't woken up when he'd started banging, so it wasn't that they were really asleep.

He couldn't think about it, so instead, he hammered all the nails back to where they should have been in all the unoccupied booths. When he got to the booth where Tom and Edgar lay slumped over a table, he stared at the exposed nails for a moment, then stuck his hammer into his pocket and walked away.

No sense in going through the effort of moving them if this was a dream, and he'd wake up in the morning with nothing done. He glanced at the empty booths, their backs firm against the wall again, and smiled in satisfaction at a job well done.

Even if he hadn't fixed everything, he'd made one thing better.

He looked around the tavern, taking in the dim, cozy room that he spent the vast majority of his time presiding over.

The Lucky Goat was his home, and someone had come into it and turned his sanctuary into a prison.

Beastie let out a whine as she made her way toward the kitchen, and Roan turned to follow her. Abigail was probably there and would let her out, but he was curious if whatever had stopped him from leaving through the front door was also effective on the back. He walked through the swinging door just in time to see Beastie head out the back.

Abigail looked back at him, her eyes bright, and she smiled. "Did you get the booths fixed?" she asked.

"I did." He nodded toward the door. "That one works for you?"

Abigail nodded in confirmation. "I haven't tried the gate in the fence, though. I suspect it'll be the same as the front. I'm just glad that we can let Beastie out."

Roan grunted. "I'll try the back gate."

As he made his way toward the door, Beastie came bounding back with a brightly colored ball in her mouth. Roan knelt as Beastie dropped it at his feet and picked it up to inspect it, dread filling his gut. "This is..." he began, turning to Abigail, who nodded again.

"The same ball," she said quietly.

Roan stood and tossed the ball back to Beastie, who settled in the corner and began to tear it to shreds.

"I knew this was a dream," he said.

"I hope it is," Abigail said quietly.

"You don't think so?" Roan said. It wasn't really a question.

"I'm afraid it's a curse," she said, the words barely a whisper.

"But magic isn't real," Roan said.

Abigail simply raised an eyebrow. "I'm glad that you think that," she said, "but I'm afraid it isn't true."

"How could it not be true?"

Roan didn't want the answer, so he simply stomped out through the back door to inspect the garden.

This was a dream. Magic wasn't real. He was simply dreaming about the ball that Beastie had destroyed last week.

He leaned down, picked up a stick, and threw it over the back fence, muttering a curse under his breath when it hit some invisible wall and bounced back toward him.

That wasn't what he wanted to see—he wanted to see it sail straight over.

And the ball was here, and it was the same ball that Beastie had destroyed last week.

Had the owner of the ball made a second one to throw over his fence and lose again?

Things couldn't be repeating like this in real life—this had to be a dream.

He marched indoors and informed Abigail it didn't work before making his way back to his office.

He could have tried the gate, perhaps, but he didn't feel like using his body to discover if the barrier existed there, too. He'd already gotten hurt too many times.

His head was beginning to hurt again, whether from the magic that had been pointed at him or the effects of being knocked unconscious, he wasn't sure. But he didn't usually feel pain in his dreams, and Abigail seemed so certain that it wasn't one.

If it was a dream, it was a beastly dream.

He clenched his teeth as he glanced around his office.

What did he need to do if this was, in fact, real, and he wasn't going to wake up in the morning with all of this behind him?

What steps were important to make sure that he and Abigail would make it through this experience?

First, he needed to get all those sleeping men out of his tavern. He didn't want to stare at them for however long this might take—the idea of them sitting there in a peaceful slumber while he and Abigail lived and worked around them was entirely unappealing.

But he couldn't shove them outside, and he couldn't put them through the front door. He could maybe put a couple of them into the pantry, but then Abigail would have to see them.

In the storage room, however...that could work.

How many men had been in the tavern? There had been seven or eight, perhaps.

They would fit in the storage room, and if they woke up, it wasn't as if they could do too much damage there.

Yes, the storage room would work.

He marched out of his office and poked his head into the kitchen. "Can you help me move them?" he asked.

"You want to move them?" Abigail's eyes widened in surprise. "Are you sure that's a good decision?"

"I don't see any other option," he said, "unless you want them sleeping around us the whole time we're trapped here."

Abigail shook her head. "No. I was just thinking how eerie it was," she said. "And I don't want any more of them falling like Conrad did."

"Conrad fell?" Roan asked.

"I kept his head from hitting the floor," Abigail said, wincing. "Though I couldn't catch the rest of him. That was when I looked over and saw you."

Roan grimaced. He hated that she'd seen him in such a vulnerable state. "We're moving them into the storage room."

He turned on his heel and stalked out into the tavern.

She could follow him or not. He didn't care.

He ignored the traitorous part of him that was glad when she followed.

They started with Conrad, since he was closest to the storage room, and they carefully carried him in and laid him against the wall.

Conrad, he could have carried on his own, but the others would be heavier.

The storage room was even darker than the main room, and full of things they wouldn't need without any customers. It was a good place to keep the sleeping men until they woke again.

Conrad was young and lean; the others proved a far more worthy challenge, and it took both of them straining to carry Edgar, who spent entirely too much time sitting in his tavern with a drink or eating instead of being active.

They moved on to Tom. Roan scooped him up into his arms like he would carry a baby—not that he had any experience, but he'd seen his brother do it a few times—and heaved upward.

The man was perhaps even heavier than Edgar, or perhaps Roan was simply exhausted already.

Abigail reached underneath to also support Tom's weight, her arms settling just inside his, and if they hadn't had a sleeping man cradled between them, the pose might have felt intimate.

It only felt awkward.

"I wasn't planning on doing this today," Abigail said, her voice straining just as much as she was as they shuffled awkwardly into the storage room.

The man's arm fell off his chest, landing solidly against Abigail's.

"I'm sorry," Roan said, not quite meeting her eyes.

"It's fine," Abigail said, though her tone suggested otherwise.

As they entered the storage room, she quickly stepped back, allowing the arm to fall and hang freely instead of resting against her bosom. Roan grunted as he tried to carefully set Tom down, his face probably as red as the beets lined up on a nearby shelf.

But he couldn't blame her for stepping back.

The rest of the men proved easier, though more than one of them put them in an awkward position. "I suppose it's a good thing none of them were awake when they were touching me, or you'd be tempted to throttle them," Abigail said with a slight giggle as he set down the last man.

Roan nearly dropped the man to the ground before whirling around to stare at her. "Has that happened here?" he asked, the words pouring out of him unbidden.

If someone had hurt her in his tavern, they would pay.

"No, no," she said hastily. "I mean, there have been times before, but not here. No one would dare to do that here—not when you and Beastie have made it perfectly clear that they're all expected to leave me alone."

She'd experienced it...but not here.

At least there was that. Roan nodded curtly, then strode out into the main room. "If anyone ever needs a reminder of that rule, you tell me," he said over his shoulder. "I want this to be a safe place for you."

He didn't dare voice the rest of the words in his head. That he wanted this to be a safe place for her because even though she had only been here a few months, she was the best barmaid he'd ever had, and he hoped she would never leave.

Saying that would be far more vulnerability than he ever intended to express to her, especially after she'd already seen him unconscious on the floor.

"I appreciate that." She'd followed him out, and something in him was glad. "I'll get our supper. It'll be ready soon," she said, smiling up at him before bending over to pick up the white rose on the floor. Roan couldn't tear his gaze away from it as she picked it up. She smiled down at the bloom and extended her hand to offer it to him before wincing and examining her thumb, where a small pinprick of blood had appeared.

A twinge of concern hit him and Roan frowned. "You ought to be more careful," he told her, swiping the flower from her before striding off toward his office.

This whole situation was highly inconvenient, and she had this bizarre way of making him feel things he didn't want to feel.

He didn't want to feel any more emotions.

All he wanted was to break this curse and figure out how to make his tavern make money again.

He joined her in the kitchen after a little while and they ate dinner in silence. Roan said nothing more to her except, "You'll sleep in here. I'll sleep in my office."

Abigail nodded, and he left the kitchen.

There were no late customers and no extra mess to clean, so he worked on the bookkeeping a little longer before he reached for the blanket he kept in the closet of his office.

He was preparing to bed down on the floor when he realized there would be no blankets in the kitchen, and Abigail would be sleeping on nothing.

His conscience and duty to her as a woman and his employee fought with his selfishness, but in the end, he brought the blanket into the kitchen. Abigail was curled up in the corner, her dress tucked around her feet, and her hands folded under her head as a pillow.

Moonlight streamed in one of the large windows in the kitchen, illuminating her face.

She was beautiful.

And staring at her while she slept probably made him a creep.

Roan sighed and gently placed the blanket over her before returning to his office, lying down on the floor and staring up at the ceiling.

Beastie flopped down next to him, and he leaned into her warmth. The sooner he fell asleep, the sooner he could wake up to find that this had all been nothing more than a dream.

Chapter Four
Abigail

Abigail rolled over, her head bumping against something hard, and she opened her eyes.

Oh.

She was on the kitchen floor in the tavern.

It hadn't been a dream.

There was only a little light coming in through the windows, so it was still early, but she wouldn't be able to fall asleep again.

She sat up, stretching blearily. It had not been a good night's sleep. Her whole body ached, and she'd tossed and turned for far too long.

A worn woven blanket with fraying stitching around the edge covered her legs, and Abigail frowned, fingering the faded cream fabric. Had Roan come in to bring this to her? She hadn't heard him at all—he must have come in after she'd finally succumbed to sleep.

Part of her had been afraid that if she fell asleep, she wouldn't wake again, trapped in the sleeping curse that inflicted the other inhabitants of the tavern. She shuddered at the reminder of carrying their sleeping bodies into the storage room.

She'd dreamed of less safe times, of men who hadn't been sleeping when they'd brushed against her in ways that were less than appropriate.

Not since she'd come here, though.

She'd never felt safer than when she was here with Roan and Beastie.

Even if it was highly improper for her to be the only one awake here with him...she knew he would never harm her.

However, sleeping on this floor another night might.

Perhaps there were things in the attic that might make their situation more comfortable. She'd heard a rumor there were things up there from when his grandparents owned the tavern—perhaps there would be more blankets.

She took a deep breath and stood to start the kettle of water for tea and oatmeal, folding the blanket and tucking it out of the way on a shelf. She had a busy day ahead of her, and breakfast would set her up to have a good day.

Roan was right. If they were going to be trapped here, they might as well accomplish the things that they never actually got to do because they were too busy taking care of the tavern patrons.

She reached for a spare handkerchief and used it to tie her hair back. Today she would tackle dusting. It hadn't been done in far too long, and taking the broom to the heights of the tavern would make a mess of her hair if she didn't cover it.

Perhaps she could let in some light, too, by taking down the heavy curtains and cleaning them. It might make the time pass faster and keep her spirits up if there was more light in the building.

She understood why Roan kept the tavern dim. It made the tavern warm and cozy, welcoming in ways that it wouldn't be with the sunlight streaming in.

But she did miss the sunshine when she was in the main room.

Fortunately, her kitchen had large windows, and she'd never closed the curtains on them. She stopped at the sink and raised her face to the light, taking a deep breath. Today was going to be a good day.

The tea kettle began steaming, and she quickly prepared tea and oatmeal before loading a tray and making her way to Roan's office. Would he be awake this early? She rarely came in this close to dawn, but she didn't know what his habits were.

She would knock, and if he didn't answer, she'd leave the tray for him.

Her stomach felt odd as she approached his office. She'd never felt this uncomfortable before, but then again, it wasn't every day her employer covered her with a blanket while she slept.

It was perfectly normal for her to feel odd about that.

She knocked and waited for him to call, "Enter," in a rough voice before she did so. She balanced the tray on her hip to open the door, and when she entered the room, she looked around before finally spotting him.

He was lying on the floor, his head resting on Beastie's side, his hair tousled and his clothing wrinkled.

"I brought you breakfast," she said, glancing away from him. It felt improper to see him in this way, even if he'd seen her in a similar state.

He had no blanket, and the fact that he'd given it to her made warmth fill her chest.

Had anyone ever done anything like that for her before?

At least he had Beastie to snuggle with.

"I'm sorry. I didn't think you would still be sleeping," she said as she set the tray on his desk.

"I don't normally sleep this late," he admitted as he sat up. "I suppose the effects of being knocked out yesterday caught up to me."

"Do you feel well?" she asked, hurrying over and taking his face in her hands to inspect his eyes. "I should have thought to look at you for side effects. I apologize for not thinking of it."

Roan seemed flustered by her nearness, and after seeing that his eyes looked normal, she took a step back. "I apologize. I ought not to have been so forward," she said, a blush spreading across her cheeks. This situation was so odd.

"No apology necessary. Are you trained in healing?" Roan asked.

Abigail stood and reached for the bowl of oatmeal, handing it to him before sitting back down on the floor, a safe distance away from him. "I learned a few things from one of the women I grew up with. One of the things was that after someone hits their head, you should check their eyes to make sure they look the same."

"And what do you do if one is different?" Roan asked dryly, putting his spoon into the oatmeal, but not eating anything.

"Make them rest," she said. "Lots of water and rest. Soup can be helpful, too."

"And soup fixes an eye?" he asked, his eyebrows quirking in disbelief.

Abigail laughed. "Soup fixes everything."

"If you say so." His tone remained dry, but there was a lightness to him that she was not used to. Was it almost a smile?

This was too strange.

"Come on, Beastie. You want to go outside?" she asked, suddenly desperate to escape. Beastie scrambled to her feet and followed Abigail toward the kitchen, where she let her out into the back garden.

Soup could fix most things, but it couldn't fix the awkwardness that had sprung up the moment she'd run away.

The curtains were disgusting.

Abigail eyed them, chewing on her lower lip as she took a deep breath.

The ladder was in the storage room.

The dust and dirt collected on the curtains was enough to choke a human...but the ladder was in the storage room.

Where all the sleeping men were.

Reaching out to run a finger down the curtains was enough to make up her mind, though.

They had to be cleaned.

She sighed and walked toward the storage room. Roan hadn't come out of his office all morning, and if she didn't know better, she'd think he was hiding from her.

If she were braver, she'd ask him to help her get the ladder...but she wasn't brave, and facing the sleeping men was less intimidating than knocking on his office door. So she opened the door, quietly, almost as if she was going to wake the men.

It was silly. She wanted them to wake up, wanted them to come back to life, and yet she couldn't help tiptoeing through storage to where the ladder hung on the back wall.

She didn't look at any of their faces. They hadn't changed. Everyone's eyes were closed, their breathing normal—though more than one of them was snoring. She choked down laughter as one of them hit a particularly out-of-tune note in the cacophony of song that was the snoring.

Hefting the ladder onto her shoulder, she carried it out of the storage room, carefully stepping over the few stray limbs that had splayed out from where their respective owners lay.

If only she could wake them up by stepping on them.

As it was, she didn't want them to wake up with unexplained bruises.

The bottom end of the ladder whacked into someone and Abigail grimaced.

Maybe one or two bruises.

She made her way to the front of the tavern, where her least favorite curtains were, long and heavy drapes on all the windows.

They had their reasons for existing...but they had been annoying her from the moment she first started working here. The only reason she hadn't taken them down yet was because she had been afraid of making Roan upset—and because she'd never had time.

But now she had time, and if he was upset, he could put them back up later, on his own.

At the very least, she could give them a good beating.

It might improve her mood, too.

She hummed a merry tune to herself as she propped the ladder against the wall and climbed it to begin taking them down.

The curtain weighed more than she'd expected, and the ladder wobbled as she released it from the hooks holding it above the window. She froze, gripping the top rung with shaky hands, but it didn't fall.

Abigail quickly found a rhythm, and by the time she had reached the northern wall, she had a large pile of drapes to clean sitting in the middle of the room.

The whole room was brighter. She could see the dust flying through the air—and the fact that she could see the dust meant there was sunshine.

The sunshine made it all worth it.

She moved the ladder for the last time, leaning it against the wall between the final curtain and the Lucky Goat tapestry that Roan's grandmother had made. Climbing to the top, she took a moment to study the tapestry.

It was beautiful. The stitching was immaculate, featuring a goat, the tavern's name, and a border of tankards and white roses with green leaves. It must have been a true labor of love.

But it was torn.

Abigail frowned at the rip in the embroidery.

What had happened to it?

Not that it mattered—she could fix it.

If there was one thing she knew, it was how to be handy with a needle and thread. Her father had never been much for sewing, so the role had fallen to her as soon as she was old enough to hold a needle. She'd stitched up his clothes over and over, with him ripping them over and over again.

How he got into so many situations that involved tearing his clothes, she wasn't sure, but he did.

Mending the tapestry would be easy compared to attempting to hold together fabric that was so worn you could almost see through it.

She released the last curtain from its hooks and dropped it to the floor before turning her attention to the embroidered sign. Clearly, Roan's grandmother had been an incredibly talented seamstress to create such fine work.

The tear was small, but it was toward the top where the tapestry hung, which meant the weight of the fabric was pulling on it and would inevitably cause it to rip more.

She couldn't let that happen.

Taking it down to fix it was the best option, and no one would even notice the tear once she put it back up.

Abigail reached over to begin unfastening the tapestry, letting go of the top rung of the ladder to use both hands.

"Abigail!" Roan's voice barked.

Her concentration slipped, and so did she.

She wobbled at the top of the ladder for a moment, the ladder itself bobbling back and forth. Fear shot through her heart as she realized how far she was from the ground. She scrambled to grab the ladder again, but her hands met nothing but air, and she fell, trying desperately to reach it.

A strong pair of arms caught her just before she hit the floor, and she stared up at Roan, her eyes wide, her arms wrapping around his neck involuntarily.

She could hardly breathe.

She clutched him tighter as the gravity of what had happened flooded through her. She could have seriously injured herself, and with the two of them trapped here, there would have been no help.

"Thank you," she whispered.

"What were you doing?" he asked, setting her down so abruptly it nearly felt like he threw her. "What makes you think you're allowed to touch my grandmother's tapestry?"

"I was going to mend it for you," Abigail said, finding herself growing flustered.

He was upset. Why was he upset with her?

"Don't touch my grandparents' things," he said, the words harsh as he turned and stalked away. "And I'm not paying you to help while the tavern isn't open."

"Did I ask you to?" she called after him.

Roan paused, turning on his heel to stare at her.

Why had she said anything? She didn't like to confront people...but there was no one to witness this, and perhaps saying something now would be better than living with just him and his attitude for however long it took to break this curse.

"I haven't said a word about wanting to be paid," she said, taking a step closer to him. "And I'm only trying to help you fix the things that have been put off for too long, as you said you were doing. Perhaps you would rather I sit and do nothing while we're trapped in a curse, but I, for one, would prefer to be busy, and I wish we could get along with each other while we're here."

She took a deep breath and nodded firmly at him before turning back to pick up the pile of curtains.

He waited a moment before he left again, his footsteps quieter than normal on the floor.

Something had been different this time. He was usually gruff, but this outburst felt more personal. Maybe there was a reason the tapestry was hanging so high up on the wall, if he didn't want anyone touching it. Had somebody else torn the tapestry, and he hadn't known how to fix it?

It didn't matter. Even without mending the tapestry, she had plenty to do without trying to make sense of Roan's behavior.

Cleaning the curtains took most of the day, and it was growing dark when she finished with the last one. She hadn't washed them, since that task was better suited to two people with how large they were, but beating them out in the garden had taken out huge quantities of dust.

Putting them back up would have to wait—if she put them back up at all. The sunshine that flooded through the side windows as the sun set was the prettiest thing she'd seen in this building since she'd set foot in it.

She set the curtains to the side; they might make a cozier nest than curling up on the floor of the kitchen as she had the night before.

Her gaze flickered to the attic entrance in the ceiling. A blanket would be cozier than the curtains. Were the rumors true? Were there things up there from Roan's grandparents?

And more importantly, was there a blanket?

She reached for the ladder, which still leaned against the wall. She hadn't put it back in the storage room, not wanting to walk over the sleeping men again.

It was eerie walking amongst the men she knew from their loudest, most vivacious moments, now lying on the floor in a space of stillness.

She leaned the ladder against the wall beneath the opening to the attic. Gathering her skirts in one hand so she wouldn't trip on them, she began to climb up.

There would be no falling this time.

When she reached the top, she eased the panel up and over the lip and poked her head through the hole, glancing around.

The rumors had been correct. She grinned as she looked around—there was a spinning wheel in the far corner, and a few wooden crates were scattered around on the heavy beams that supported the ceiling.

What was in them, though?

Abigail climbed through the hole in the ceiling and stood halfway. It wasn't tall enough for her to stand fully, but fortunately she could walk without being entirely bent over. She stepped carefully, making sure to stay on the beams so she didn't fall through to the floor below.

No more falling.

"Now where did you go?" she heard Roan exclaiming from beneath her, and then the sound of him climbing the ladder. Beastie whined from the floor.

"What are you doing in the attic?" he asked. But this time, the words weren't harsh.

"I'm hoping there will be an extra blanket, so I don't have to try to force you to take yours back," she said pointedly. His face colored lightly, which was interesting. She hadn't thought that pointing out the way he had given her the blanket would embarrass him.

"I didn't need it," he said quickly.

"But I'm sure you wouldn't complain if we were to find another one up here," Abigail added with a teasing smile.

"I wouldn't," he admitted. "And I'm sorry."

Abigail smiled at him, and the air around them felt warmer. This was a start. "I forgive you," she said quietly.

"I'm still not paying you while the tavern's not open, though." There was a different tone to his words, and she decided to ignore it for now. She could try to parse it out later.

"I know," Abigail said, smiling sweetly at him. "I'm helping anyway. We're stuck here, so I might as well."

She set her lantern down, but he picked it up and handed it back to her, taking over the task of lifting the lid off the crate.

"It's clothing," she said, frowning at the dress sitting on top. That was unexpected.

"These were my grandmother's things," he said. "When my grandmother passed away, my father didn't want to get rid of them, and my mother didn't want them, so he put them up here."

"He decided to put them in an attic instead of sharing them with someone who might be able to use them?" Abigail asked. The more stories she heard about Roan's father, the less inclined she was to think much of the man.

"When you put it that way," Roan said, "it does sound rather odd."

"Can't imagine putting such things where they can't serve any purpose," Abigail said as she fingered the rich fabric of the dress lying on top. It was a beautiful pink, probably very expensive. "I would have died of happiness to have a dress like this when I was younger."

"Well, you can have it now," Roan said, glancing around the attic. "It's not doing any good up here. Let's bring it down."

Abigail could hardly find words to speak. "You're sure?" she asked.

"I'm sure," he said, glancing up and down her frame critically. "You'll have to take it in. My grandmother was a hardy woman."

"As opposed to my frail frame?" Abigail teased. She was not a heavyset woman, though she was no waif. Not anymore, at least.

"Any women's clothes in there are yours to do with as you like," Roan said.

"You don't think your wife might want them someday?" she asked, the words slipping out before she realized.

She glanced up at Roan, and it was her turn to blush red. "I'm sorry. I didn't mean—"

"You make a good point," he said before she could try to explain herself. "But I think it unlikely that the future Mrs. Alder would even know these were here in the first place, and we could use them now. And if all you want to do is turn them into blankets for orphans, I don't care. Nat has just as much right to them as I do, I suppose, and I'm sure someone at his orphanage could use them. They always have need."

He stared down at the crate pensively, and Abigail cocked her head. "Do you want me to dig and see if there are any of your grandfather's clothes here, too?"

"I doubt there are," he said with a shrug. "My father had no issues taking what he wanted from my grandfather." He put the lid back on the crate and moved on to the next one, as if to say that the topic was closed, too.

Inside were a set of teacups and a teapot, a beautiful collection with pink roses decorating them.

"Your grandmother must have loved roses," she said, taking a cup out of its straw nest and looking it over. There was a small chip in this one, and the sight made her smile. They were clearly well-loved.

"We used to have tea parties with them," Roan said, the words falling out like he couldn't contain them. "Before my father found out."

Abigail looked up at him in surprise, the bitterness of the words a strong contrast to the fondness of the sentence before it.

Had he had a difficult relationship with his father, too?

"Bring it all down," Roan said, waving his hand. "It does no one any good up here, and bringing it down makes far more sense. It's one more thing we can go through while we're stuck here."

"Did you give up on fixing things in the front today?" Abigail asked. "I've hardly seen you at all."

"I was going over the books," he said, dragging his hands down his face. "Not that I made much progress. It seems all they do is frustrate me."

"I could help," Abigail offered.

Roan glanced at her and frowned. "I'm not paying you to help with the books," he said.

He was clearly hung up on the payment issue.

"You don't have to pay me," Abigail said. "I'll help anyway."

Roan eyed her curiously, then shook his head. "Let's just get these out of here," he said.

They dragged all the crates to the edge of the hole in the ceiling, and Roan made Abigail go down first for modesty, before climbing down onto a rung near the top himself.

Beastie whined and Abigail reached for her and patted her head. "Don't worry," she murmured to the dog, even as she worried herself.

He stood at the top of the ladder, reaching up into the hole to grab a crate, passing them down to Abigail.

"Be careful," she said as the ladder began to wobble on the fourth crate.

"I'm fine," Roan muttered. "Stop worrying about me."

Worrying about him was most of her job, but perhaps it was best not to point that out. She took the fifth and final crate from his hands, and he disappeared into the hole one more time before returning with the lantern.

They gathered near the first crate, which only held his grandmother's clothes. Beastie wormed her way between them, sniffing each item as they took it out and inspected it.

The second crate held the tea set and a few other fine dishes—far too fine for the tavern. The men would break them instantly. "We should give these to your brother, if he can use them," Abigail announced as she put the tea set back.

The third crate held some books, which Roan announced could be given to the town's new library, and the fourth crate held tools and kitchenware.

"Last chance," Roan said as he pried off the lid of the final crate.

Abigail squealed in delight as a large patchwork quilt and what could only be a down-filled quilt appeared.

What a luxury! She dove into the crate and pulled them both to her chest, taking a deep breath. "And somehow they don't smell terrible," she announced, as if it was the most important fact in the world. She took another breath and their smell improved yet again.

Roan shook his head as if annoyed by her antics as usual, but the motion didn't carry the exasperation it usually did.

"I'll take my blankets back," he said. "You can have these ones. They're much too fine for an oaf like me."

What?

Abigail turned to him. "What do you mean, an oaf like me?" she demanded. "You are not an oaf. On the contrary, you are, and have always been, a gentleman. And I'll thank you to not disparage the man who has treated me with such kindness."

Perhaps he was rough around the edges, and he didn't have a way with words, but he had a heart underneath that beat true, and that was something she didn't take for granted.

Surprise lined Roan's face as he stared at her. Then he nodded.

"I'll take your warning to heart," he said. "Thank you for your kindness."

He turned and walked away, and Abigail stared after him. It was her turn to be surprised. Where had that come from? And why had he acquiesced so easily? That was unlike him.

But she didn't have time to think about it.

She had food to make for the two of them, and a nest to make for herself.

Tonight was going to be a much better night.

Chapter Five
Roan

Beastie whined as Roan stood and pulled his shirt over his head in one easy motion, throwing the dirty one to the floor. She grabbed the shirt in her teeth, carrying it over to her corner.

"Don't rip it," he warned her as he reached for the extra shirt he kept in his drawer.

It was a good thing they'd found his grandmother's clothes in the attic. It meant that Abigail would have something to wear while they washed their dirty clothes. He'd help her do that in the morning.

Before he could put his clean shirt back on, there was a slight knock at the door, which opened easily. The latch hadn't clicked shut.

As it opened, Abigail stumbled in to see him standing shirtless at his desk.

"Oh!" she exclaimed, hiding her face in the crook of her elbow despite the blanket she carried. "I'm so sorry," she said, turning around. "I'll come back later."

"There's no need," Roan said quickly, pulling his shirt on and crossing the room before she could leave. "Thank you for bringing the blanket."

"Of course," she said, not quite willing to meet his gaze, her cheeks a stunning shade of pink.

Had she always been so beautiful when she blushed?

Roan shook himself mentally before walking away from her and setting the blanket on his desk.

"And thank you for dinner," he added.

She looked up at him in surprise. Did he forget to thank her for food that often? Was it really that rare for him to do so? If it was, he ought to feel ashamed, because Abigail was the best help he'd had in years, and making sure that she felt appreciated should be one of his main tasks.

"And I'm sorry for snapping at you earlier," he said. He'd already apologized once, but even if he couldn't find it in him to explain why just yet, she should know that he was sorry.

"I forgive you," Abigail said, her gaze quickly falling again. Though the pink was fading, the flush still remained, and something in him felt a sense of satisfaction at the thought.

He was almost enjoying this.

The feeling was unsettling. He had been alone for so many years that the idea of enjoying spending time with anyone—not to mention a woman—seemed far-fetched.

But in this moment, he was almost content, if he dared to say it.

"I'll, uh, I'll just go," Abigail said, gesturing toward the door as she began to inch backwards.

He cleared his throat. "I hope I didn't make you uncomfortable with my state of undress."

"Oh, no," Abigail said, pausing, though she still wouldn't look at him. "I used to see my father all the time."

Roan glanced at her skeptically. "I don't imagine seeing your father without his shirt on made you unable to look him in the eyes," he said dryly.

Abigail turned pinker, but she looked up at him, and there was merriment in her eyes. "I suppose you're right," she said.

"You don't need to be uncomfortable," Roan assured her. "Unless I've done something?"

"No, I just—" She looked at him. She looked down his body, and her words came out a bit strangled. "You don't look anything like my father did."

Roan grinned and couldn't help flexing his muscles for a moment under his shirt. She must have seen the movement, because she turned away to hide her face with a light giggle.

"I'll stop," he said, resisting the urge to chuckle.

"You'd better," she said as she hurried out the door without saying anything else.

Roan looked down at Beastie, who seemed entirely unamused by everything that had just happened, while he couldn't stop grinning.

"Well, Beastie," he said, "that was fun."

And he hadn't had fun in longer than he could remember.

Soft music filled the air as Roan opened his eyes. He blinked in surprise as he looked around the room. His tavern had never looked cozier. Candles were lit on most surfaces, there was the smell of fresh bread and warm soup in the air, and Lyle stood in the corner playing his fiddle.

All the men currently asleep in his storage room were scattered throughout the room, as if nothing had ever happened. Roan shook his head, blinking at the sight of them, lit in a rosy glow that filled the whole tavern.

Was this a dream, or was everyone being asleep the dream?

"I don't know what's happening," he muttered, rubbing his hand over his face. Beastie bounded toward him with that dratted ball in her mouth. Hadn't he seen her destroy it twice already?

"It's good to see everyone awake, isn't it?" a soft voice said behind him. Roan turned to see Abigail, and his jaw dropped. She was wearing his grandmother's pink gown, which fit her perfectly.

So this was a dream, then.

Abigail was good, but she was not able to tailor a dress for a woman of his grandmother's size to fit as if it was made for her in only a few hours. Not when she'd also been cleaning curtains and preparing food for both of them, while he hid in his office and pretended that he wasn't looking at her differently than he ever had.

"You look beautiful," he said. He wasn't quite sure where the words came from, but they were true, and he wouldn't take them back. She did look beautiful.

"And you look handsome," she said, smiling at him.

Roan looked down to see himself wearing one of his grandfather's old coats, one that he remembered Grandmother turning into cleaning rags after it became too ratty to be worn anymore.

Definitely a dream.

"I haven't seen this in years," he murmured, running his hands over the buttons. Like her dress, it fit him perfectly, which was a surprise given his grandfather's stout nature.

"It seems we're meant to enjoy ourselves tonight," Abigail said, looking around the room with a smile. "Everyone looks happy."

"Well, I can only hope that their bodies aren't starving to death while you and I get no closer to figuring out what to do to break this curse," Roan muttered.

Abigail smiled winningly. "I know," she said, "but for a moment, could we forget it and just enjoy ourselves? I've never worn a gown this fine, and it seems a pity to waste this moment in fear and doubt, when that fear and doubt will be there for us in the morning, just as surely as it is here tonight."

Roan looked down at her and nodded, doing his best to hide how afraid he was. "Of course, my lady," he said, offering a hand.

She looked at him in surprise.

"We do seem to be dressed up," he pointed out, "and there is music."

"Are you asking me to dance?" Abigail said, her eyes wide.

"On the contrary, I—well, yes, I suppose I am," Roan said, though he was just as surprised as she was. Where had this notion come from? Dream Roan was apparently bolder than he gave himself credit for.

"I would love to," Abigail said. Her eyes shone brightly as she accepted his hand and he swept her into a dance. Perhaps dream Roan was on to something, though, because Roan couldn't remember a time when he had felt more free as he pulled Abigail into his arms and into a dance.

"You can dance?" she asked in surprise as his arm wrapped around her waist and he started twirling her around in a dance.

"I can," he said. "My mother always thought that we were better off than we were and seemed to think that the local nobility would be inviting us to their events. So she had Nathaniel and I learn how to dance."

"Did you ever go?" Abigail asked.

"Not once," Roan said dryly as he twirled her out and then back in. Her eyes lit up every time he did so, and he found himself captivated by it.

When had she become so beautiful? This was Abigail, for heaven's sake. She was his employee, and he owed it to her to remain professional. But as the occupants of the tavern cheered them on while they twirled around the room, Roan couldn't quite find it in himself to remain professional when all he could see was her.

She even smelled good, he noticed. He'd never quite gotten close enough before to realize she smelled like lavender and honey, and he fought the urge to lean in and take a deep breath of her hair. What did she wash it with? They'd been trapped here long enough that any scent she'd worn should have faded away.

"We'll figure it out," she promised him, meeting his eyes with a determined look. "I know you're worried. I am, too, but I know that you and I will figure it out. We're too stubborn not to."

"I worry for them," he said, looking around the room at all the people he spent most of his time with.

Abigail closed her eyes and reached up to press her finger to his lips as she whispered, "Shush. That's a problem for the morning."

Her finger was warm against his lips.

Her eyes opened wide and she immediately pulled her hand back, trying to pull away from him.

He didn't let her.

"I'm sorry," she began to say, but Roan shook his head.

"Don't be." His voice was rough, and he couldn't get anything else out.

But she couldn't regret that. He wouldn't let her.

She turned pink and nodded, but she didn't say anything else.

The song finished then, and they pulled away from each other to applause from all the men in the tavern.

"Go back to your drinks, you fools," Roan said, as Abigail blushed and looked away shyly. He didn't need her feeling self-conscious, not when that dance had been the most wonderful moment he'd had in years.

Now he just had to convince her to do it again.

Chapter Six
Abigail

The morning dawned bright and early, and Abigail's peace was disturbed by a wet nose sniffing in her ear.

"Good morning, Beastie," she said with a sigh as a wet tongue began to lick her face. "I don't suppose I could convince you to let me sleep for another twenty minutes?" she asked.

No such luck, as the dog padded toward the back door, having successfully woken her.

Abigail sighed and got to her feet, heading toward the back door and opening it to let Beastie out to do her business, leaving it cracked open so she could let herself back in.

Maybe she would convince Roan to use this time of forced productivity to finally put in a swinging door for Beastie that didn't require a human. It wasn't really a problem, since Beastie usually went home overnight with Roan, where they had such conveniences—she would assume—or Roan had to deal with it, not her. But this week had only proved to highlight the fact that Beastie needing to go out was an inconvenience that they could remedy relatively easily, with just a little bit of work.

And Abigail was all about doing just a little bit of work to make everything easier, especially when it could potentially allow her to get a few extra moments of sleep.

Not that she wanted this to last forever. In fact, hopefully they would break the curse soon and everything would go back to normal.

But just in case.

She stretched her arms wide and yawned as she made her way to the stove to stoke the fire so she could heat the kettle and make herself tea.

Perhaps today she could avoid walking in on a shirtless Roan. Her cheeks heated at the reminder. Maybe instead, she could find him wearing the blue coat he had worn in her dream last night.

It had been a grand coat, though it hadn't compared to the pink dress she'd been wearing in her dream. She grinned to herself as she reached for the tea set from the crates and began washing two of the cups. It was silly to be so excited over a dress one had worn in a dream, but in her defense, it was a gorgeous dress.

Any girl would be privileged to wear it...and as soon as she tailored it, she'd be able to wear it for real.

It was hard to believe that Roan had given it to her. And if it wasn't enough for him to give her a dress that was clearly sentimental for him, he'd shown up in her dream last night and danced with her.

Her cheeks heated at the thought. It had been a wonderful dream and would have been even if he hadn't danced with her. The tavern had been full of light and laughter, and it was everything she had ever wanted for the tavern—

Not that it was her place to be dreaming about the Lucky Goat that way. The tavern was Roan's, and she needed to remember that.

But it had been magical, seeing it come alive in the way she had so often thought it could.

The kettle heated before she'd washed the rest of the tea set, so she pulled out the old teapot and two mugs before the kitchen door swung open and Roan walked in.

"Good morning," he said gruffly.

That was different.

"Good morning," she said with a smile on her face. "I hope you slept well."

"I slept as well as can be expected," Roan said with a grimace, "though I did have a better dream than I usually do."

Abigail eyed him warily. Had they shared a dream last night? She'd heard of such things happening to people who were caught in a curse together.

"What happened in your dream?" she asked, hoping that she sounded nonchalant.

"You were in it," he responded.

"Oh?"

The door swung open and Beastie loped through, bounding toward Roan and pressing her head against his hand for attention.

"Yes," Roan said. "You were there, and we danced."

"That's funny," she said. "I had the same dream."

Roan pretended that he didn't find that extremely interesting. She could tell because instead of saying anything, he rolled up his sleeves and moved to the sink.

Abigail tried not to stare at his forearms. When had forearms become so interesting? It was only because he was about to wash dishes, she assured herself. That's why it was so interesting—not at all because she was captivated by how his muscles moved.

"You're washing dishes?" she asked. That was her job.

"I thought that since the only people you've been cooking for have been you and me, maybe I ought to help with something," he said. "It's not as if I'm taking care of cleanup out front, and I know cleaning is your least favorite job of everything you do here."

Abigail tried not to warm at the thought that he'd paid that much attention to her favorite and least favorite jobs.

If he kept being so nice, she was going to start falling for him, and that was not something she needed right now.

"You've been so helpful with the cleaning over the past year, I've forgotten how much work it was—how much I did—until you took it over for me. And I'm not going to lie to you, I don't miss it at all."

He laughed, and Abigail stared at him in shock. Roan laughing—she'd never thought she'd live to see that day.

He stopped laughing when he saw the look on her face. "What's wrong?" he asked.

"You were laughing," she pointed out.

He had the decency to recognize how unusual that was, because he didn't ask further.

He sighed and reached for another dish, plunging the teacup in his hands into the soapy water.

"I know I can be a bit of a beast sometimes." He paused, pulling the cup out and staring at it. "It's how Beastie got her name, you know."

"I… I didn't know that," Abigail replied. She cocked her head at Roan and waited for him to continue as she grabbed a towel and took the cup from him to dry it.

"I was raised primarily by my father," Roan said. "He was worse than I am, and I know it doesn't excuse me, but it's why I am the way that I am. When I was growing up, sometimes some of the other boys would call me a beast and say that none of the girls would ever want to marry me when there were other options for them. And everything I experienced since then seemed to support their taunts."

Abigail's heart hurt for the child that Roan had been. No child deserved to be taunted like that.

"So I thought, when I got Beastie, that perhaps she could make that memory sting a little less." Roan wouldn't meet her eyes as he handed her a wet bowl. "I think it worked, but it doesn't change the fact that I know I'm still a beast at times. So I thought maybe I could help with the dishes for once."

"Well, you've never been a beast to me," she pointed out. "And I think those boys were wrong." Her ears began to burn with embarrassment as she realized what she had just said. "I mean, I suppose they were wrong—not that I want to marry you, but I wouldn't not want to. I mean, it's not as if you're so bad that I couldn't marry you. It's just that...you know, you're my employer, and I shouldn't be thinking about marriage when it comes to you, and I would be silly to even think about it." She cut herself off as Roan looked at her in amusement.

"I'm not trying to trap you into marriage by sharing woeful tales of my childhood," he said, "so no need to fret."

"As long as nobody realizes that I spent all this time alone with you and all those other men," Abigail said lightly, the realization sinking in that it might be exactly what everyone thought if they found out about this—her reputation would be in tatters.

But maybe Beastie's ball had been an example of the fact that they had gone back in time, and perhaps no one would notice, except the six men who would hopefully wake up in the storage room...though perhaps they could convince them it had merely been a batch of bad ale.

There was a loud thud as something hit one of the windows above the sink, and Abigail and Roan looked at each other. “Was that a bird?” Roan asked.

Abigail’s eyes widened. “Was it?” she asked.

A bird had hit the window two days after Beastie found the ball in the garden.

She remembered because Beastie had found it, too.

If it was...it was further evidence that they had gone back in time, as opposed to simply being caught in a curse.

But she didn’t want to talk about curses and magic right now. Not when they were already talking about something uncomfortable.

“I should hope you’re not trying to trap me, anyway,” she said, realizing the silence had gone on for far too long. “I can’t imagine why anyone would go to such lengths to force me into a marriage. Nobody has ever wanted me.” She said the words as lightly as she could.

It was true. She hadn’t wanted to marry the man her father had tried to force her to marry, but he hadn’t exactly been keen on the idea, either, and neither had any other young man before or after.

Now it was Roan’s turn to watch her uncomfortably. “You know it’s not because of you, right?” he asked. “Any man would be lucky to marry you. You're smart and kind and...beautiful."

His voice caught on the last word, and he turned to Beastie, who was lying next to him. "Did you want to go outside, Beastie?" he asked the dog, who sat up immediately at the word "outside."

So, it was his turn to use Beastie as an excuse to leave a conversation.

Abigail's lips twitched in amusement at the sight of Roan, quite literally running away from her. He could say all he wanted that any man would want to marry her, but in her experience, no man had ever wanted her—and it looked like he was included in that list.

Chapter Seven
Roan

Roan paced in the garden as he threw sticks to Beastie and waited for her to bring them back to him,

He was a fool.

He'd just called Abigail beautiful and then run away from her.

Even if she didn't think he was a beast, she certainly had no reason to assume anything good of him at this point. But if there was one thing that this time together had shown him, it was that he desperately wanted her approval and wanted her to think well of him.

In the past two days, she had gone from being simply his employee to being someone whose opinion he valued. He'd meant every word of what he said. She was smart and kind and beautiful. She had more kindness in her little finger than he had in his entire body, and he'd always known that, but he'd never been able to enunciate it so clearly before—because until now, he'd never spoken to her about anything other than the tavern.

And it wasn't as if he'd spent much time with her now, either.

But the tiny bit of time they'd spent together had proven that if he chose to spend more time with her, he could very quickly lose his heart to her, and that was an unsettling thought.

What if she didn't feel the same way? What if she couldn't wait to get out of here? What if she ran after they broke the curse and never came back?

Not that he expected she would...but there was always the potential for that, and even though he hadn't considered it until now, he was terrified of it.

He didn't want to lose her, and that had never been clearer.

The door opened behind him, and Abigail came out, wiping one hand on her apron, the other holding the bucket of kitchen scraps for the compost pile. Roan watched as she dumped the food in the pile and set the bucket down before coming over to join him.

"At least your garden is still growing well," she said, her voice steady.

Her presence was steady as well.

He looked down at her gratefully. She could have run away from him and avoided him after he'd made things awkward, but she was here standing beside him, showing him that he was not alone and that she hadn't been scared off.

He swallowed over the lump in his throat.

"I'm glad it is," he said, trying to keep his voice even. "I would have been sad if it all stopped growing because of this curse."

"I think it may end soon," she said, her voice quiet. "If we did get sent back in time like the ball suggested, we only have three more days."

"That's still a long time," Roan said, his voice shaking a little more than he would have liked.

"I know," she said quietly. "I'm worried about the others."

Roan was, too. He'd gone into the storage room a couple of times to check on them. They were still breathing, and they didn't appear to be suffering any ill effects of being asleep. But they were asleep.

“We should prepare to feed them something nutritious when they wake up,” he said. “Though without knowing when they’ll wake up, that makes it difficult.”

“I know,” Abigail said with a sigh. “But there’s some canned soup in the storage room now, so we’ll be able to open a couple of those jars when the time comes and only have to heat it up.”

She was so resourceful. Before she’d come, he’d always been living moment to moment in the tavern, and what he served was dependent on what they had. But shortly after joining him, Abigail had filled the storage room with canned foods and canned ingredients that made it possible for them to quickly feed more mouths than normal if they had unexpected visitors.

It didn’t happen often. Most of the town had their rhythms and never changed. But occasionally, they had a few extra visitors, and having the food put up ahead of time to quickly open and serve a hearty stew or a delicious soup was something he would never take for granted again.

If only he could afford to give her a raise. She deserved it.

“Thank you,” he said quietly, wondering if she would know that he meant for more than just the soup.

She smiled up at him, and his whole day grew brighter.

"You're welcome," she said, resting her hand on his shoulder for a moment before turning and walking back into the tavern.

Roan was ready to tear his hair out of his head. He had been fighting the balance sheet for the past hour and was no closer to figuring out why he couldn't make everything work properly.

The fact that the numbers didn't quite match wasn't what bothered him. What bothered him was the fact that it seemed he was losing money.

He didn't know how to stop it, but if he didn't stop it, he could lose everything.

Roan ran his hand down his face and sighed. This was not what he'd been hoping for. When he sat down to work on this, he'd been hoping to find that he had miscalculated and would be able to work it all out. Instead, he found more bills that he didn't remember paying, and more vendors than he could expect to pay with the usual number of patrons his tavern hosted on a regular basis.

It all seemed rather hopeless, and he didn't like hopeless.

"I don't know what I'm doing wrong," he said to Beastie, who was sitting at his feet, staring up at him. "I feel like I should be better at this, but I'm not, and I don't know how to fix it."

It wasn't a new problem. He'd first realized it was bad last winter, when he'd started trying to court Beatrice, the librarian. That hadn't gone well, of course—who could ever learn to love the town beast? All it had done was convince everyone that a beast was all he was.

His grandparents had been a team—his grandfather doing the day-to-day running of the tavern, and his grandmother doing all the behind-the-scenes work, including the accounting.

He'd hoped that he could find that, too.

When Montgomery, the town's trader who went back and forth to the capital city regularly, had mentioned that his daughter was one of the smartest in town, he'd thought she might be worth pursuing. He couldn't afford a wife he couldn't trust with his money or his tavern.

And getting her away from her drunk of a father also seemed like it might be appealing.

Montgomery had even started hinting—or saying outright—that he should court her.

But Beatrice had run off and married the lord who started her beloved library.

Roan didn't begrudge her the happiness she'd found, but it had left him, once again, in the position of not knowing where to look for a wife who could put up with being married to him and his tavern.

And still losing money faster than he could earn it.

Beastie simply laid her head down on her paws and stared up at him with those big brown eyes that trusted him to do everything. Roan sighed. Beastie and Abigail were depending on him, and he had to figure this out for their sake.

Giving up was not an option.

"Yeah, we'll figure it out, right, Beastie?" he asked, reaching down to scratch the top of her head.

She thumped her tail against the ground enthusiastically, and Roan smiled at her. At least somebody here loved him.

He frowned at himself. Where had that thought come from?

There was a rap at the door, and he said, "Come in," his heart feeling lighter when he looked up at Abigail.

Somehow, she had become someone who could lift his spirits just by entering the room, and he wasn't sure he liked that.

It sounded dangerously close to "love" territory.

Even when he'd been at the height of attempting to court Beatrice, he'd never been in love with her.

The last time he'd loved another human...well, it had ended a long time ago, and he wasn't sure he wanted to be that weak again.

But he could hardly tell her to leave, even if he wanted to.

"Is something wrong?" she asked as she approached with a tray that held a bowl of stew and a slice of bread that smelled divine.

"Maybe," he admitted. "I'm not sure I can make these numbers work right."

Better to admit to that than the fact that he was wrestling with his feelings.

"Can I help?" she asked as she slid the tray onto the table next to him. "I used to help my father when he had trouble making the numbers work."

Roan glanced at her. "Really?"

"Of course," she said. "Do you truly think I would lie about that?"

"No," he said hastily. "You just surprise me with all your many areas of expertise."

"I'm a well-rounded woman," she said with a smile, fetching the extra chair in the corner of his office and pulling it up next to his desk. "Show me what's wrong with these numbers."

Roan handed her the book, slightly surprised that he was willing to do so.

If Conrad had suggested he let Abigail look at the tavern's numbers, he would have laughed at him, but suddenly, the idea of her helping him with it didn't seem odd at all. In fact, it felt completely normal.

"I think I see at least one issue," she said after a few moments of staring at the numbers. "You are still paying the baker for more loaves of bread than we purchase. We reduced our order when I started baking some, but it looks as if the price hasn't gone down since then."

He looked at her in a new light. She hadn't even looked at it for five minutes, and she'd already seen an issue that he had overlooked for some time.

"And I'm sure there are some other things we can cut back on if that's an issue," she said, leaning closer to the page in front of her to study it. "I know there are other things in the kitchen that we could buy less of since I've started doing some of our own preserving."

Roan could hardly keep the emotion out of his voice as he said, "Thank you."

Abigail looked up from the notebook and smiled at him, and Roan could scarcely breathe. "Of course. It's in my best interest to make sure the tavern does well," she teased.

Roan's mouth opened to say something, but then he closed it.

She was dangerous. One smile from her had him ready to do anything to see that smile again.

He needed to guard his heart, because if he didn't watch it, he was going to fall head over heels for her. He needed her to run the tavern—he couldn't lose her because he decided to be silly and let his heart get involved.

That wouldn't help anyone.

He just had to convince his heart that leaving her alone was the better option, because right now, it was treacherously close to doing anything for her.

He sighed and looked down at Beastie, who was looking at him in disapproval. Love was not for him. It was for those who weren't trying to run a successful business. He needed all his wits about him to make sure that he didn't lose his tavern, and falling for Abigail was a distraction he could not afford.

Women in general were far too easy to lose one's head around. He'd gone to drastic measures to keep his brother from losing his heart—he should be willing to do the same to protect his own.

The argument felt hollow, but it was the best he could do at the moment as he thought of his brother and the woman he had loved—perhaps still loved. Roan wasn't sure. He had distanced himself from the situation after Thea had appeared in the Northlands, ten years after Nathaniel had left her behind in Riyel.

Neither of them knew that Roan had taken their letters, and he was no longer sure if it had been the right decision. He'd thought it was the right thing at the time, or he wouldn't have done it.

There was no sense in regretting it now. It was over. It didn't matter if he wasn't sure it was the right thing anymore.

His brother had gotten over his broken heart far more quickly than he would have without Roan's intervention, and that was the whole point of why he had done it.

Love wasn't worth it.

The only things he could count on were his never-ending pile of work and Beastie.

He didn't need a woman interfering with all the things he had to do, even if she smelled like flowers, smiled like sunshine, and had a knack for fixing his problems.

Chapter Eight
Abigail

Abigail watched as Roan shut down before her eyes. The smile on his face disappeared, and his mouth closed as he looked down at Beastie.

What had changed his mind? She'd thought for a moment that she would see the Roan she knew was hiding in there somewhere, but he was gone again.

She bit back her sigh of frustration. She had a couple more days to get him to come out of his shell before they caught back up to time, if she was right...and oh, how she hoped she was right.

She didn't want to think about the alternative.

"Enjoy your dinner," she said as she got up from her seat and left his office. Beastie came padding after her, and

Abigail let her out, following her into the dusk. She had been working hard today, and a moment to enjoy what was left of the sunset felt like a necessary reward.

She had organized the pantry today, so she wasn't lying when she'd told Roan there were a few things they could stop purchasing. From what she'd seen of the records, the tavern was not doing well financially, which explained some of why Roan was so taciturn and unforgiving. If all he did was worry about the state of the tavern, it wouldn't leave him much time for anything else.

But she couldn't help wondering if he'd lost so much joy for another reason. Why did he shut down any time he tried to have a moment of fun with her? What was his reason for letting no one but Beastie close to him?

She made her way back into the kitchen, where she puttered around cleaning until Beastie asked to be let in.

Her mind was still buzzing with *what ifs* and she didn't want to sleep, but Beastie would wake her early in the morning, so perhaps it was for the best if she did. She was curled up in her nest, having finally settled enough to become drowsy, when the door creaked quietly, and soft footsteps followed. She opened her eyes just enough to see Roan creeping in with a small candle and his dirty plate from dinner.

She smiled to herself at the picture he made before noticing the candlelight flickering off his bare chest.

Looking away would be the proper thing to do.

But perhaps she wasn't always proper.

With no one to witness her impropriety, she allowed herself to take a moment and look at how finely shaped he was while he poured himself some water. She'd met many men while wandering with her father and in the course of her time at the tavern—some burly, some brawny, some slender, some...not slender.

Roan looked like the kind who worked hard and enjoyed it but didn't spend all his time concerned with the way he looked.

That was her favorite kind.

She closed her eyes and heat flooded her face. She shouldn't be looking at Roan like that. He was her employer and looking at him like that was not something she should be doing...even if he looked fantastic.

And having thoughts like that were certainly not proper.

She squeezed her eyes shut tighter as he walked past, hoping he wouldn't see that she had looked at him.

"Good night," he whispered quietly as he left the room.

She didn't answer.

The tavern was filled with joy when she opened her eyes, that rose gold light giving everything an extra glow. The fiddle played again, the drinks poured freely, and no one was in a bad mood. Even the old men sitting at the back table were being talkative.

Conrad sat in his usual place at the end of the bar, and he smiled as she refilled his tankard.

"Good evening," he said. "Did you have a good day?"

"I did," Abigail said. "It was fine." Perhaps it had been a confusing day, but a good day nonetheless, and she didn't need to burden Conrad with all her difficult feelings regarding Roan. He had no business hearing all of it, and frankly, she didn't want him to think badly of Roan when Roan hadn't done anything wrong besides being awkward, which wasn't really his fault.

Well, it was, but it wasn't.

She settled on saying, "It was a fine day."

Conrad raised his eyes. "You already said that," he pointed out.

"Oh, I did." Her cheeks turned pink. "I apologize. I'm scattered tonight."

"That's allowed. What's on your mind?" he asked.

"Not much," Abigail said, even though that was a complete lie. There were a million things on her mind—whether Conrad and the others were going to be okay after this curse was over, whether she and Roan would be okay, if Roan was going to ask her to dance again in this dream world—or if she should be brave enough to ask him.

She couldn't imagine being bold enough to do that herself, but perhaps it would be the only way to get him to dance with her again. She'd been surprised that he'd done so the first night, and she wasn't sure he'd do it again.

"I see you're far away," Conrad said.

Abigail flung a towel over her shoulder and moved down the bar, away from Conrad and his way of seeing right through her. "I suppose I am," she said, looking down. "It's been an interesting couple of days."

"I'll say," Conrad said. "I don't think I've left the tavern in three days."

Abigail raised an eyebrow, hoping he'd elaborate without her having to say anything.

"I'm sorry—I don't know why I said that," Conrad said with a laugh. "It's just an odd feeling that I had. Also, you changed your dress back, which is probably why it feels like it's been longer than a day."

Abigail looked down at herself to see she was wearing her usual brown dress and white apron. "I thought I should stop playing dress-up," she said with a laugh.

So Conrad had been in this dream world the whole time. She needed to tell Roan. Where had that man disappeared to?

"If you'll excuse me a moment," she said, turning around and hurrying toward Roan's office.

But before she could knock on the door, it opened and he strode out, colliding with her at full speed.

Before she could fall, his arms came around her and pulled her close, holding her up while she regained her balance.

"Missed me that much?" he asked, before the light in his eyes faded. He let go of her and took a step back, clearing his throat. "I'm sorry. What did you need?"

Abigail wanted to tell him not to be sorry—that she felt safer in his arms than anywhere else, and maybe she could trip again, and he'd catch her a second time.

But she didn't dare.

"Conrad has been awake in this dream world since the curse began," she said quickly, before she could do something so silly as that. "He thinks it's been one day and I simply went and changed my dress."

Roan looked down at her dress, then his eyes flipped back up to her face.

"So this is a dream world," he said, "and you and I are here in our sleep."

"Yes," she said, "but not in the daytime."

"Do you think if we feed them in this dream world, it would make a difference?"

Abigail shrugged. "I don't know, but it certainly doesn't hurt to try." She took a step away from him before she did something like fling herself at him to feel his arms around her again. "I'm going to the kitchen, and I'm going to take a can from the pantry, and in the morning, we can see if it's still there."

"I don't know if that's how it works, but it's worth a shot," he said with a nod. "This magic is strange."

Abigail didn't know either, but the magic required to weave a spell like this was far greater than any she'd been exposed to before.

It wasn't even taught to those who had access to dragon eggs.

"It's a dark magic," she said quietly, the words tangling in her throat.

Roan stared at her, a flicker of fear in his eyes before they became hard once more. "After we feed them, you and I need to talk about how you know that this is dark magic."

He lowered his voice and asked, "If you don't mind?"

The words were stuck in Abigail's throat. As much as she wanted to tell Roan, she didn't want to tell him. She didn't want him to know where she'd come from, and how she had been raised. But Roan wouldn't hurt her—she knew that—and he deserved to know.

"Later," she promised, before turning on her heel and hurrying to the kitchen.

She had soup to prepare.

"Come on, Abigail," Tanner said, rolling his eyes as she stood over him, her wooden spoon in hand. "I'm not hungry."

"I don't care," she said sweetly. "It's a new recipe. I need everyone to try it, to tell me whether they like it or not."

And if she had enhanced the soup slightly to make it irresistible to eat—well, that was no one's business but hers.

And maybe Roan's.

But what he didn't know wouldn't hurt him, and if they already had to discuss magic later, adding one more thing to confess wouldn't make a difference.

"Or maybe I'll just never feed you again." She let the words trail off in a sickly-sweet threat.

"Oh no," the boy said, his eyes wide as he picked up the spoon and took his first bite. "I'll try it."

Abigail grinned.

She'd had a feeling that when faced with the threat of no more meals at the Lucky Goat, Tanner would cave.

They all had.

She looked around the room at all the nearly empty bowls and nodded in satisfaction. Either she would wake up in the morning to dirty bowls in the sink and an empty jar, or she would wake up to nothing, and the bitter feeling that despite her past, she might be failing the men in the tavern—men she felt responsible for.

She looked over at Roan, who was watching them all eat with grim determination on his face.

She wasn't the only one feeling responsible—Roan was anxious, too. If only she could ease his burden. She made her way over to him and stood next to him in solidarity. She might not be able to ease his worries, but at least she could be there so he would not be alone.

"This needs to work," he muttered.

"It will," she said, reaching out to take his hand and squeeze it.

It felt completely normal to hold his hand.

It shouldn't have.

But it did.

She pulled her hand as if to take it away, but he squeezed tighter, not letting go, and she watched as he swallowed hard. Maybe she imagined it, but she could almost see the tension easing in his shoulders.

He could hold her hand if it eased his burden.

"Thank you for being here," he said quietly.

"Any time." She meant it. She would be here anytime for Roan and these men.

She owed more to Roan than he could ever know. She had been given a place of her own where she could stand on her own two feet and be strong, and that was something she had never gotten from her father.

She looked up at Roan, who squeezed her hand again in response, and looked back out at the tavern.

This was her home now.

She would go back to sleeping at the inn when the curse broke, but the Lucky Goat was her home.

She had fought the title for the past year, telling herself it was silly to care so much about what was only a job. But it was no longer just a job. Whether she wanted it or not, the Lucky Goat and Roan meant more to her now, and she could not escape that no matter how she tried.

Lyle pulled his fiddle out of the corner, and all eyes turned to the two of them, mischievous grins on every face.

"Dance, dance," Tanner began chanting.

"No," Roan said, but Conrad came around the counter and pushed the two of them out from behind it with a twinkle in his eyes.

"You're in so much trouble," Roan muttered to Conrad, who simply laughed as he pushed the two of them into the center of the floor.

"You'll have to deal with it," Conrad said.

Abigail stood still, her hand still held loosely in Roan's, and looked up at him. Was he going to refuse, or would he dance with her again?

His eyes softened as he looked down at her, and he offered his other hand without letting go.

"Shall we dance?" he asked, and the tavern erupted into cheers.

Abigail smiled and took a step closer, allowing him to wrap his arm around her waist.

"I love dancing," she said.

As the fiddle struck up a merry tune, Abigail allowed Roan to twirl her away, and for a few moments, let herself forget they were stuck in a curse together.

As the song came to an end, Conrad was there with an outstretched hand. Roan relinquished his hold, and maybe it was just her imagination, but it felt like he didn't want to. She felt a thrill run through her at the thought—if only it was true.

Conrad twirled her around the floor amidst cheers and laughter from the rest of the men in the tavern, and Abigail let loose and let herself just have fun.

Dancing with Roan was enjoyable, but right now the two of them didn't know what they were, and that added a level of caution to their dancing. With Conrad, it was different, and she could just have fun.

The dance came to an end, and the next man was there. Before the night had ended, Abigail had danced with all of them. As she finished her dance with Stumpy, the last man, Abigail took a deep breath and grinned.

"That's everyone," she announced. Her cheeks were flushed from exertion, and she was ready to collapse into a chair.

Then Roan was there, holding out his hand.

"One more?" he asked quietly in his deep voice.

Abigail couldn't keep herself from smiling up at him as she placed her hand in his and nodded to Lyle to play one more song. But instead of the fast songs he'd been playing all evening, he settled into a slower song that almost felt like a lullaby.

Roan pulled her into his arms, and she immediately relaxed into them. She'd been wrong. She didn't have to be cautious when she was dancing with Roan.

She could completely trust Roan with whatever happened, and as he slowly led her in circles around the room, Abigail couldn't stop smiling up at him.

This was not what she had expected from the evening, but she couldn't think of anything more wonderful.

Chapter Nine
Roan

Roan woke up and rolled over, his neck stiff from lying on one side most of the night. Beastie was still insisting that he use her as a pillow, and while she was softer than the floor, she was taller than his pillow. His neck was unaccustomed to sleeping at this angle.

At least he'd had a good dream again.

He had vague memories of Conrad dancing with Beastie, holding her front paws in his hands, and Stumpy insisting she could dance on her own.

But the memories of dancing with Abigail were anything but vague—he could practically still feel her in his arms, how warm and alive and vibrant she was as she laughed when he twirled her out and back into his arms.

He swallowed hard. If only those moments weren't a dream—he would love nothing more than to dance with her in the real world.

Had she had the same dream again? Would she remember the way they'd danced? Or the way they'd fed the men–

He scrambled to his feet, throwing the blanket off and reaching for his shirt, pulling it on as he hurried toward the kitchen. He had to know if the soup was gone.

Abigail was already up, using her apron to grab the handle of the kettle so she wouldn't burn her hands as she prepared tea for the two of them.

"The soup?" he asked.

Abigail lit up like the sun itself. "It's gone," she exclaimed. "It worked."

"And you know what I'm talking about," Roan said, more to himself than to her.

"I know," she said, her eyes sparkling. "The dream world is real and we're actually interacting with them in it. So we don't have to worry about them dying. They may be malnourished by the end of this, but if I can force enough soup into them every night, it might be enough."

If anyone was capable of force-feeding them enough soup to keep their bodies alive, it would be Abigail.

Roan slumped against the counter as he accepted a cup of tea and murmured "Thank you. Good morning, by the way."

Abigail chuckled. "Good morning. I had the same thought this morning. That's why I'm awake before Beastie got to me."

Roan looked down at the tiny teacup cradled in his hands. It was from his grandmother's set, the one she'd found in the attic.

He hadn't used it since they'd lost his grandmother and his father had packed away every memory of her that he could. Memories flooded through him: tea parties just because they could, sharing a cup of tea while they baked together, the way she hadn't scolded when he'd chipped one of them.

A sip of the tea brought back even more memories. He'd kept his grandmother's favorite stocked since her death—one of the few things his father hadn't taken—but drinking it out of the teacup brought images of laughter and love he'd long since forced himself to forget.

The memories had been locked away for so many years, but Abigail had come into his tavern and changed everything, making his life brighter and happier.

How could he repay her for that?

He couldn't.

He watched in amusement as Beastie bounded in and went straight to Abigail, rubbing against her skirts with her giant head.

"Apparently I'm useless now," he said, as his dog threw herself all over Abigail.

"It's just because I feed her," Abigail said with a grin. "You have to go outside first," she told the dog, who trotted over to the door immediately when she heard the word "outside."

Abigail opened the door for her and closed it, shaking her head affectionately as she returned to her cup of tea.

"That dog is going to be the death of me one of these days," she said.

"She loves you, though," Roan said as he drained the rest of the tea in one swallow. Was it a child-sized teacup, or was he just that much bigger than the last time he'd had it?

"I was thinking today I can tackle the garden beds that need to be repaired," he said. "Unless you have something else that needs to be done first."

Abigail shook her head. "Unless you want to make a swinging door for Beastie, that's a good task for today. I was planning on mending and adjusting your grandmother's dress this afternoon, but if you want, I could come help you outside instead. It might be nice to get out in the sunshine."

"I would be glad to have you help," Roan said, his voice thick. He would, which was odd—normally he preferred working on his own. "And if you have time this afternoon, I'd love to look at the budget with you a little more closely and see what else we can cut back on."

Not that he actually wanted to do that...but he needed to do it, and having her there would make it more bearable.

"I can do that," she said with a smile. "I'll just put a big pot of soup on this morning so I don't have to think about it later."

"And tonight we can give it to them again." And hopefully they would wake up soon.

She nodded. "It's interesting that we've been awake this whole time in the dream world. I don't know what that means for the curse."

"Maybe it means that you and I are the ones who are dreaming," Roan said. "Are we dreaming these days in between? Is this whole part—is this whole thing—a dream?"

"I don't know," Abigail admitted. "I know more about magic than most, but this is not like the magic I know."

Roan crossed his arms over his chest and looked at her, waiting for her to say more. She looked down at her feet, her hands fidgeting in her apron.

"Perhaps we could discuss this while working on the garden beds?" she asked quietly. "I would prefer to have something to do with my hands while we talk."

Roan nodded. "I'll get my hammer."

The sun beat down on them as Roan and Abigail knelt next to one of the raised garden beds, the warmth welcome after the slight chill in the air. Roan's grandfather had built the garden beds for his grandmother, and ever since, they had slowly been deteriorating.

Fortunately, Roan had gotten a pile of wood from one of his patrons as payment for a tab he couldn't settle in coin. He'd been intending to use it to fix the garden beds, but he'd never had time. All his waking hours were spent serving customers or doing the necessary work to run the tavern.

"If we're the ones in a dream," he said to Abigail as they began to pry an old board off, "do you think all the work we're doing will stick?"

Abigail grimaced. “I hope so. It would be quite the disappointment to wake up to find it all still needing to be done.”

Roan let out a coarse laugh. “It would be a cruel trick, is what it would be.”

Abigail was quiet for a moment. “I’ve probably enjoyed this more than I ought to,” she admitted quietly. “It’s been nice to catch up on these jobs without having to worry about customers, and even sleeping on the floor hasn’t been as bad as it could have been. I could do without all the stress, though. If it wasn’t for that, I would say we should have the sorcerer send us back in time once a year so we can catch up on everything.”

“Is that what happened then?” Roan asked.

She didn’t say anything for a moment.

Had he pushed for too much, too quickly?

“I don’t know,” she said softly. “I’ve never seen this before. I grew up in a hidden community of magic users. We lived in the mountains to the north, where the king and his anti-magic laws couldn’t reach us. But living up there came with problems. The growing season was too short, and we couldn’t grow enough to supply ourselves. It had been one thing when magic was tolerated in Galamere and our people could come down and trade for what we needed—or at least, that's what they told us."

She paused as if she wasn't sure what else she could reveal.

Roan couldn't quite believe what he was hearing. There was a whole community of people who used magic? Did she use magic? And why was she here?

"I was supposed to marry a man down here. My father arranged it all. He was trying to take care of me," she said, her fingers curling into the dirt beneath her palms, "but he didn't do it well."

Roan's heart nearly stopped. Was she married? Or spoken for?

"The marriage didn't happen. It all ended up being rather disastrous, actually, and I'm not sure where my father went after that. But that's why I'm here, on my own, and why I know things about magic. It's why I know that whatever spell was used to do this is more than is normally taught, and I'm afraid it means whoever used it is dabbling in a black magic that ought not to be used."

She shivered and Roan fought the urge to put his arm around her shoulders. She didn't want comfort—she wouldn't even meet his eyes.

"I don't know who the sorcerer who cast this spell was, or if I even know them. We had to abandon our home when I was young and my father and I became nomads, which is why sleeping on the floor doesn't bother me." She let out a dry laugh. "I just hope that whoever cast the spell knew enough about what they were doing to give us a proper out. You don't remember anything else, do you?" she asked hopefully.

Roan shook his head. He'd been racking his brain ever since that day when he woke up, with no memory of the actual curse happening.

"I wish I did," he said. "All I remember is hitting my head. I do have a question for you, though."

He hammered a new board into place. He could feel Abigail waiting beside him but wasn't quite sure how to word it. How did you ask a question that could possibly be incredibly offensive? But he had to know.

"I hope this isn't a bad question to ask," he said quietly, "but are you able to do magic?"

He leaned over to grab the next board to avoid making eye contact.

Abigail let out a small humph. "I wish I was," she said. "I'm not talented enough to do real magic. I can enhance things, which made me a valuable commodity as a child, until I stopped allowing myself to be used by people for the express purpose of amplifying their magic. But I can do things like make the tavern a more welcoming place, or make the soup taste more delicious, or anything like that. It's useless in most cases, but a man like my father found it a very useful skill, until I realized what was happening. I—"

Roan looked over at her. She was looking down at the garden bed, avoiding meeting his gaze, but he still saw the tear that fell from her face into the dirt.

"He used me until I stopped letting him, and then he tried to marry me to someone down here. I'm sure he had some underlying reason that I don't know, but to me, it felt like he no longer had any use for me. Since I stopped letting him use my talent to enhance his own magic, he was only trying to get rid of me."

She cleared her throat. "When that fell through, I ran away from him. I don't know where he is now, but I know that I don't want to see him again."

She still wouldn't meet his gaze, and he couldn't blame her. Baring her heart to him had to be terrifying—especially since she'd just admitted to using small magic in his tavern in a country where magic was illegal.

In her place, he'd be scared, too.

Roan reached over and lifted her chin gently until she looked up at him.

"You are so much more than just a tool to amplify someone else's skills," he said. "You say it's not much, but since you came here, you have changed everything in my life for the better."

The honesty behind the words surprised him—he meant every bit of it.

"I hope that you never think I'm only using you for your talents, but I do want you to know how much I appreciate them, Abigail."

Abigail smiled, and he dropped his hand, unwilling to admit how much he liked touching her.

"You say that now," she said with a self-deprecating grin, "but I'm sure someday it'll wear off."

Oh no. Did she really believe that?

Roan set down his hammer and shifted on his knees to take both her hands in his.

She had to know better.

"I know that after what you've been through, it must seem like there's no one in your life you can trust to not use you for your magic. But I didn't even know you had it until just now," he pointed out. "And if you'd asked me yesterday, I would have said the same thing. I hope you realize that you are worth so much more than just the skills you bring to the table. You're truly the sunshine in this place, and I hope you always will be."

She sniffled, but before she could say anything, Beastie came bounding up and skidded into them.

Roan grabbed Abigail as she toppled sideways, pulling her into his chest with one arm, flinging out his other to block the dog that had barreled into them at top speed.

"Down, Beastie!" Roan said, pushing her away from Abigail. "Don't you dare knock Abigail over. You know better than that."

Beastie sat, looking properly chastised, with a stick in her mouth. Roan reached over, took it, and threw it, sending the dog bounding away again.

"She didn't mean to knock us over," Abigail said softly, looking up at him.

Her hands were resting on his chest like they belonged there.

"I know," Roan said gruffly. "I just didn't want her to hurt you."

He didn't want anyone or anything to hurt her ever again.

Not Beastie, not her father, and certainly not him.

"Thank you," Abigail said, pulling away from him, resting her hand on his arm for only a moment before turning back to the garden bed. "Now, let's get these beds finished so we can go tackle the budget. I don't know that my magic will be any good there, but who knows, maybe I can enhance that, too."

Roan turned back to the garden bed, as she wished, but glanced at her out of the corner of his eye.

"I'll be grateful for anything you can do," he said, "whether or not you're able to help."

"I wasn't able to help my father, but I can certainly try to help you." Abigail smiled in his direction before looking back down at the dirt with a quiet sniffle.

If her father ever showed up, Roan would be having a word with him.

Nobody was allowed to make Abigail cry—but certainly not the man who was supposed to protect her the most.

Chapter Ten
Abigail

A TEAR DRIPPED OFF the end of Abigail's nose onto the pink dress from the attic.

She hadn't planned on revealing so much of her past to Roan in the garden...but now that she'd started thinking about it, she couldn't stop.

Roan had been so sweet about the whole thing, which was something she never would have expected from him. And the fact that he, of all people, had reacted that way proved that her father had made bad decisions.

If Roan was so upset on her behalf about something he couldn't change, what would he have done if he had been there when she told her father no for the first time?

She thought back to the moment she'd refused to hold her father's hand as he prepared to cast a spell to make their host forget that he hadn't offered to send them away with two of his sheep. If there hadn't been witnesses, she wasn't sure what her father would have done.

As it was, he cast the spell, knowing it would only last for a few minutes, and they had run off with both sheep instead of the one the man had promised them in return for her father's work.

She'd stood her ground after that, even though she wasn't able to leave him yet. He'd always told her that she was lucky to have him, that a young woman with no family or useful skills couldn't survive on her own. But after the marriage he had tried to force her into had failed, and he had been run off, she'd used that freedom to escape him—hopefully forever.

And now she had a place where she belonged, and Roan, who seemed to think that she belonged here, too. It was so different than the way she'd grown up, and the fact that he didn't shun her because she had magic lifted a weight off her shoulders that she had hardly realized was there.

If someone had asked her if she felt worried that Roan would find out her secret and make her leave, she would have said yes—but no one had asked. She had grown so used to keeping it secret that she hardly thought about it anymore. And since her magic was not the kind that required fancy spells, a wand, or potions, it was fairly easy for her to assume no one would ever know.

But Roan knew now—and he hadn't turned away. In fact, he had come closer. He'd taken her hands in his and held them so tightly she had almost believed he would never let go again.

He'd pulled her close, and if she hadn't pulled away, he might have let her stay there in his arms.

She couldn't let herself stay, though.

Being that close to someone who accepted her...it was too scary.

A fresh wave of tears came until she could hardly see the needle and thread through them. She'd never been accepted just for being herself before, at least not since she could remember.

Perhaps her mother had loved her unconditionally, but since she'd passed away when Abigail was no more than a toddler, she didn't remember.

The kitchen door opened and Abigail sniffled, attempting to wipe the tears away before Roan could see them. But then he was there, dropping to his knees in front of the stool she sat on, concern etched across his face.

"What's wrong?" he asked, taking the dress and the needle and thread from her, setting them down on the floor, and taking her hands in his.

Abigail couldn't get words to come out, so she just shook her head.

"Hey, tell me what's wrong," he said, his thumb gently rubbing circles on her hand.

"This whole time, I thought you were just a grumpy miser, and you're actually wonderful," she choked out through her sobs, and then, realizing what she had said, she began to sob harder. "And now I'm insulting you."

Roan laughed and rose up on his knees to wrap his arms around her and let her cry on his shoulder.

"Oh, darling," he said, rubbing circles on her back. "You didn't insult me. You're right. I am a grumpy old miser. You heard me yell at Beastie earlier, and you were right, she didn't deserve it."

Abigail sniffled and nodded. "She didn't."

"But that's who I am, or who I have been. Until you came along, I shut everyone out and only focused on how the tavern wasn't doing well, instead of focusing on the things that were going well and how wonderful my life actually is. You're not wrong, and I'm sorry that it took this experience for me to realize that I should be doing things differently, but I'm not sorry that this experience brought the two of us closer together."

"Me neither," she managed to choke out as she started hiccupping. "Of course, I have the hiccups, too," she said miserably. "That makes—" *hiccup* "everything—" *hiccup* "better."

Roan laughed and pulled back enough to wipe the tears away from her eyes with the pad of his thumb.

She hiccupped again.

"You don't need to cry," he said, "but if it makes you feel better, then cry all you want."

At his words, the sobs began anew.

Her father had always told her to stop crying. Roan didn't seem to mind, though.

Hiccup.

Roan laughed and pulled her close once again. Slowly, Abigail felt her sobs subsiding as Roan's steady presence filled her senses with peace.

The hiccups took longer.

Eventually, she lifted her head from his shoulder, a quiet giggle spilling out at the sight of the wet spot on his shirt. "I'm sorry," she said, fanning air at it.

"Don't worry, I have plenty of shirts to wear at the moment," he said dryly.

Abigail's lips turned up in a quiet smirk. "I did wash your other shirt yesterday," she pointed out.

"Do you want me to take this one off so you can wash it, too?" he asked.

"That's not necessary," she said primly, though she could feel the heat flooding her cheeks. "It will dry."

"Are you sure?" He reached for the back of his neck and slowly began to peel the shirt over his head.

"I'm sure," she exclaimed, throwing her arms around his neck and holding the shirt onto his shoulders.

As much as she wouldn't mind seeing him without again...that was a temptation she should avoid. And being this close to him without a shirt on seemed like a step too far for her reputation, even if no one saw it.

She would know it had happened.

"If you say so." He let go of his shirt, his hand coming back to rest on her waist.

She began breathing faster as he stared into her eyes, as if he was reading into her soul.

If she didn't know better, she might guess that a new spell had been cast, one that prevented her from looking away from him. It was impossible, even as he looked down at her lips.

The air between them felt heavy, and her heart felt as if it might beat out of her chest.

Beastie yipped as she came into the room, and the spell was broken.

Roan pulled away so quickly, she would have felt slighted, had she not also been afraid to stay close.

She couldn't kiss Roan.

But she missed his arms around her.

"I see you're working on my grandmother's dress," he said after a moment. "Does it fit you yet?"

"Not nearly as well as it did the other night," Abigail said with a slight laugh. If only that part of the dream had stayed real.

Roan picked up the dress and held it out, assessing it. "Perhaps it would look better if you made it blue."

"Do you have any idea how much that much dye would cost?" she asked. "Besides, I like the pink, and I love the way it looks. I just need to make it fit me."

"I did tell you my grandmother was a hefty woman," he said, his lips turning up in a smirk.

"You did," she admitted. "But I'm making progress on it. I need to try it on again soon to see if these seams I'm sewing are working, or if I have to take them out and try again."

"Do you need help?" he asked, then turned red. "I mean, over your other dress, if that would be helpful, or not." He closed his eyes and heaved a deep breath. "I don't know how dressmaking works. I'm going to go."

He pressed the dress into her arms and hastily turned, but his feet were caught up in the extra skirt of the dress and he tripped. He fell, catching himself with one forearm before he squashed Beastie, who had come up behind him.

Beastie yelped, Roan hollered, and Abigail started laughing at the spectacle of it all. "I'm sorry," she said as Roan glared up at her from the floor.

She set the dress down and reached out a hand to pull him up, but instead of letting her pull him up, Roan pulled her down next to him.

Abigail's heart lurched as she fell, but Roan cushioned her fall, letting her land on his chest before immediately shoving her over to lie next to him, his arm under her head like a pillow.

They lay on the floor together, looking up at the ceiling, and Abigail couldn't stop giggling.

"I'm sorry," she said after a moment, "I don't know why I'm laughing. I can't stop."

"You think it's that funny that I nearly killed myself and Beastie?" Roan asked, looking over at her.

Their faces were so close, Abigail stopped breathing for a moment.

She'd never noticed how dark brown his eyes were.

"You didn't almost die," she managed to squeak out before Beastie pushed her head in between the two of them, licking Roan's cheek.

"Ew, Beastie," he said in disgust, pulling his arm out from under Abigail's head and sitting up to push Beastie out of their faces.

Abigail also sat up, rearranging her skirts to make sure her legs were covered, and looked at Roan as Beastie plopped herself onto his lap.

"What am I going to do with you?" he asked Beastie, who simply grunted as she rearranged herself to get even more comfortable. "You'd think you would realize you're bigger than me now. You're not supposed to fit in my lap anymore."

Roan rolled his eyes and leaned down to press his cheek to the top of Beastie's honey-colored head, then began stroking her back. "It's a good thing you're a good dog," he told her. Her tail thumped against the floor, and she lifted her head to attempt to lick his cheek.

This moment was everything Abigail had ever dreamed of but was never sure existed.

She swallowed around the lump in her throat and reached over to pet Beastie's head as the dog looked between her and Roan with all the love a dog could have.

"I know I don't deserve this," Roan said quietly, reaching under Beastie's chin to scratch her, "but I am grateful that it's happened, even if it took getting cursed to get here."

"I'm the one who doesn't deserve it," Abigail said, the words catching in her throat. She'd done some terrible things in her time "helping" her father, and to find herself here, feeling like she belonged...it was something she'd never expected to find.

"How about we agree that we both deserve it and treasure this moment?" Roan asked, reaching over to take her hand, even as he avoided her gaze by looking down at Beastie. "Is that a fair compromise?"

A compromise. "I suppose so," Abigail said, the corners of her mouth turning up.

If she didn't feel the headache coming on, she could almost have forgotten that she'd just been sobbing hysterically on his shoulder. This moment was pretty near perfect.

She would remember this forever.

"As long as we don't forget," she said quietly.

Roan's attention snapped to her. "What do you mean, as long as we don't forget?" he asked.

"Sometimes when a spell is broken, the person it was cast on doesn't remember everything that happened," she said, a sinking feeling in her chest.

"But you'll remember, right?" he asked.

"Probably," she said, the words bitter in her mouth. What would she do if the curse broke and Roan didn't remember that the two of them had become something different these past few days? If he went back to being the grumpy man he'd been for so long?

Could she break through his walls again without the help of a curse?

"You'll just have to remind me," he said, squeezing her hand. "I don't want to forget any of this."

As if she would feel comfortable telling a pre-curse Roan anything about magic. He probably wouldn't listen to her.

"The fact that you don't remember the curse happening is not a good sign," Abigail pointed out quietly.

"I don't care. I don't plan on forgetting any of this, or anything that's happened with you." He pushed Beastie off his lap and pulled her to her feet. "And just in case, I think we'd better make a few more memories worth holding on to."

Abigail's cheeks flushed as she let him pull her to her feet. He reached for the half-finished dress and held it open for her to step into it. "Maybe the waking memories will stay," he said. "And I definitely don't want to forget dancing with you."

Abigail could hardly believe this was real. She certainly didn't deserve this happiness, no matter what he said, but she allowed him to help her into the dress, which was a tad snug in the sleeves over her other dress. She hadn't finished the back yet, so it gaped open, and it was still far too long.

But Roan didn't care. He pulled her into his arms and began swaying with her as if there was music playing, and instead of a tavern kitchen, they were in a grand ballroom.

"This moment is far too perfect to forget," he whispered as he leaned down to press a kiss to her forehead, and Abigail wholeheartedly agreed with him.

This moment was perfect.

Chapter Eleven
Roan

Roan opened his eyes to find Conrad sitting on a bar stool in front of him. He had his apron on, a towel slung over his shoulder, and a handful of clean utensils. Apparently he'd been in the middle of doing dishes.

"I see the way you're looking at her," Conrad said. His voice was serious, which was a little unlike Conrad, especially when the topic of girls came up. "I don't know what changed today, but I think the two of you ought to figure it out. And if you hurt her, you'll have me and the rest of the men here to deal with." He took a swig of his ale and set it back down.

"I am not going to hurt her," Roan said, his eyes drawn to Abigail, who was across the room, serving a bowl of soup to Tom and Edgar.

"I know you don't plan on it, but no one does," Conrad said.

Abigail must have sensed that they were talking about her, because she turned and grinned at him.

Roan's heart skipped a beat as he put the utensils down. "She's incredible," he told Conrad.

"We know. We've been trying to tell you that since you first hired her. And you know, I think most of us are here for her," Conrad said. "Not that your congenial self isn't worth spending time with."

Roan glared at him, but Conrad continued, "She's the reason this tavern feels like home to so many of us."

"I know she is." Roan wiped his damp hands on the towel slung over his shoulder. "I want to make sure I don't lose her."

"Good idea," Conrad said. "How do you plan on doing that?"

Roan watched as Abigail made her way over to them before he could answer, sidling up next to him with a mischievous grin. "Talking about me, gentlemen?" she asked as she reached for Conrad's empty ale and refilled it.

Roan looked down at her and shook his head. He hadn't even noticed that Conrad had finished it. She was a distraction in every way possible. Fortunately, she seemed much less distracted than he was, and she was doing a fantastic job of managing the tavern despite his lack of attention.

"We were," he admitted as she came back and passed the full drink to Conrad. "He said I'd better be careful with you."

"I agree with him," Abigail said, winking in his direction as she hurried away again to help someone else with something.

Roan couldn't stop watching her.

"Oh, you've got it bad," Conrad said with a grin. "I can only hope to be that head over heels for somebody, someday."

"I hope the same for you." Roan turned to reach for the damp tankards sitting on the counter next to him and began wiping them down with the towel.

If someone could make him so happy...he had no doubts that there was someone who would do the same for Conrad someday.

Abigail had changed his life completely, and he couldn't imagine ever letting her go.

He watched as she made her way back behind the counter, setting down the empty tankards she'd taken from Tom and Edgar's table.

"You think Conrad was right, hm?"

She smiled at him and his whole world grew brighter. "Of course I think he was right," she said. "I know you're careful with everything you do."

She turned and bustled away again with fresh tankards, and Roan sighed.

He wasn't careful with everything he did.

He'd stopped being careful to guard his heart.

When he woke the next morning, Roan rolled over, and Beastie immediately shot to her feet, bounding toward the kitchen. Had she just been waiting for him to wake up?

Silly dog.

Roan pulled his shirt on and smiled—it was clean.

Abigail had washed it yesterday and returned it to him shortly before they went to bed. She was doing far more for him than he'd ever expected.

And now he had to ask her for something else.

He made his way to the kitchen, where Abigail was still on the floor with her eyes closed while Beastie licked her hand.

"No, Beastie, not yet," she whined.

"I can get the door." Roan offered, trying to hide his smile.

Her eyes shot open, and she pulled the covers closer to her chest.

"Roan," she squeaked. "I didn't realize it was so late."

"I'll just take Beastie out," Roan said with a chuckle as he followed the dog out the back door, leaving her in peace to finish getting ready for the day.

When he came back in a few moments later, Abigail was up and putting the kettle on, shaking her head at him as he entered.

"You didn't warn me," she said.

"I didn't realize I woke so early," Roan said. "Apparently Beastie really needed to go this morning."

Abigail shook her head at the dog. "You're trouble," she said, but she gave Beastie an affectionate pat on the head as she added, "I don't know what I'm going to do with you."

"Hopefully feed us," Roan said with a grin.

"I'm sure you'd like that, wouldn't you?" Abigail laughed, pointing to the bowl of millet on the counter.

"Don't worry, I'm making breakfast. It will be ready soon."

"Could I get your help with the budget today?" Roan asked. "I know yesterday got away from us."

The garden project had taken much longer than he'd expected, but he wouldn't complain, since he'd gotten to hear more of Abigail's history.

And dancing in the kitchen had been worth every second of distraction.

"Of course," she said. "I'll come to your office as soon as breakfast is ready."

"That sounds like a plan," Roan said as he closed the door and left the kitchen with Beastie in tow.

Roan was staring down at the numbers in consternation when Abigail arrived with two bowls, two mugs, and two teacups on a tray.

"I thought it might make this easier if we were enjoying breakfast while we did it," she said. "But if you'd rather, we can wait."

"No, let's get this over with," Roan said with a sigh. "I don't know what to do with this."

Abigail pulled up the chair next to him and handed him the bowl of millet. "You eat," she said, taking the paper in front of him and studying it. "These are all the expenses, correct?"

Roan spooned some into his mouth. She had mixed it with applesauce and some spices, and it tasted delicious.

"Thank you for breakfast," he said before shoving another big spoonful into his mouth.

"You're welcome, you heathen," Abigail said, wrinkling her nose at him as he chewed, his mouth barely able to close around the food. "You don't need to put that much in your mouth at a time."

"Too good to wait any longer," Roan pointed out before diving into the next bite.

"Well, I already see a couple of things we can cut back on in the kitchen," she said, crossing them out. "And I think we can probably save some money if we paid up front for some of these, if there are enough funds to do that right now. We pay later with the grocer, and I do believe he charges extra for that. He also charges extra for delivery, and it wouldn't be hard to pick things up on our way in when we are coming to work. At least, it wouldn't be far out of my way. I'm not sure which way you come from."

Roan glanced over at her. "I forgot—you don't know where I live." He suddenly had an itch to bring her to his home. "My grandfather built that house, too."

"I'm sure it's lovely," Abigail said. She wasn't really paying much attention to him, all her focus on the sheets of paper in front of her. Her nose scrunched as she concentrated. "We can definitely cut back on treats for Beastie."

Hearing her name, Beastie perked up and looked at Abigail, who smiled at the dog.

"I'm just kidding. We don't really buy treats for you. You just get food from all those people in the tavern who think they can feed you when we're not looking." Her tone was affectionate even as she added, "Lousy customers."

Roan and Abigail shared a grin.

"Conrad is so bad about that," Roan said.

"Every time," Abigail agreed with a laugh. "It's ridiculous."

"She sure does love it, though," Roan said with a laugh.

"What's not to love?" said Abigail. "She gets to get fat."

Roan reached over to rub Beastie's back, nearly falling off his chair in the process.

"She may be getting fat, but she deserves it," he said.

"Are you sure she does? I think you're just biased."

"Absolutely biased," he said with a grin. "But Beastie deserves nothing less than the best."

"Do you have any reports that show the income?" Abigail asked, not quite meeting his gaze. "If you don't mind me seeing them, that is. I am curious to see how much we need to cut, and if there are certain months—certain seasons—that do better than others."

Roan nodded. "We struggle in the summer when the men work later," he said, opening a drawer and pulling out the notebook that lay on top.

"What are those?" Abigail asked, looking into the drawer.

Roan froze when he realized what had been hiding under the notebook, and Abigail noticed, because she quickly said, "Never mind. Let's look at these numbers."

But Roan sat and stared at the pile of letters sitting in his desk, all of them still neatly sealed, all of them unread. Guilt gnawed at his stomach.

She would probably think he was a terrible human.

He had been.

"I'm sorry. I shouldn't have asked," Abigail said gently, nudging the drawer shut with her ankle. "Let's move on."

Roan shook his head.

"I did something that I shouldn't have." The words tasted like gravel in his mouth.

It was one thing to have done what he did—it was another to admit it.

The pit in his stomach at having to tell her was proof that he'd messed up.

Abigail looked up at him, waiting.

"Those are the letters that my brother and his sweetheart wrote to each other," he said. The words were hard to choke out. "But I kept them from each other."

Abigail's eyes widened. "Why?" she asked.

It was a simple question, and her tone carried no blame—only curiosity.

"I thought I was helping him," Roan said, looking down at the floor, his stomach churning. "I know now that I shouldn't have."

If she'd asked him a week ago, he probably still would have said it was for the best that he had kept Nathaniel from writing to his sweetheart, who lived in Riyel. Since she was only causing Nathaniel pain, he'd thought it was easier for both of them to forget each other and move on. Nathaniel wasn't going to leave their mother.

But now, with Abigail here—showing him how the right woman could make things easier—he suddenly wasn't sure at all.

"They lived too far apart," he said. "And Nathaniel wasn't going to leave our mother when she was sick. I thought it would be easier for both of them to forget each other and move on when we knew Nathaniel wasn't going to leave."

Abigail gave him a soft smile. "You tried to help."

"And I think I just made it worse," Roan admitted bitterly. "My father always told me that showing emotions was weakness, and I thought Nathaniel was weak for wanting her for so long. But now...."

Now he was beginning to wonder if he knew what Nathaniel had felt for Thea.

"Have you told him?" she asked quietly.

The thought of telling his brother felt like being stabbed in the gut, but he knew he had to.

"No." Roan buried his face in his hands.

"Do you think you ought to?" she asked, reaching over to rest her small hand on his knee.

The small touch was almost his undoing.

"Yes," he said, his voice cracking. "They deserve to know I was a fool. I hurt them, and I can't undo that."

"But you can say you're sorry," Abigail said softly. "And while it may not seem like enough, sometimes that's all it takes."

Roan looked over at her, and she offered him a smile that—while it didn't fix everything—somehow made it better.

"When we get out of here, I'll talk to him. I promise. And I'll bring the letters."

The thought made the knot in his chest loosen, even if the idea of admitting what he'd done was terrifying. Nat would be furious with him, and for good reason.

"Your brother is all the family you have left," Abigail said. "I think the two of you should do what it takes to become friends again. And if you need my help to do that, then I will be glad to help. If I had any siblings, I can only imagine how helpful it would have been when I was struggling with the way my father treated me. Perhaps healing your relationship with your brother might heal more than you think it will."

She took her hand from his knee and reached for the notebook. "Now, enough with one depressing topic. Let's move on to the next and see if we can't figure out a way to make you spend less time in your office."

"You don't think I'm a terrible person?" he asked her, suddenly desperate to know her answer.

Abigail sighed and looked up at him with regret in her eyes. "I've done things I wish I hadn't done, too. I helped my father do some very mean things and thought I was helping us survive. So no, Roan, I don't think you're a terrible person."

Tears filled her eyes and, while he regretted making her cry, he couldn't regret knowing that she didn't think he was a terrible person.

"I think you are a person who has been through so much more than a boy should go through, and you're doing your best. That's all we can do."

Roan found himself blinking back tears and let out a barking laugh. "Well, isn't that insightful."

She chuckled through her own weepy eyes and reached up to wipe a tear from his face. "Aren't we a good pair."

It wasn't a question, but he wanted to answer it anyway.

"Yes, we are," he said, leaning over to wrap his arm around her shoulder and press a kiss to her forehead.

They were a perfect pair.

Chapter Twelve
Abigail

The fiddle played, and the tavern patrons talked, and Abigail just enjoyed being in her element and watching Roan in his.

They were running out of time. She knew it. But until they did, she meant to enjoy this.

She didn't know if Roan would remember anything after tomorrow, or if she would, or what would happen with the curse at all. But this might be their last night, if she remembered correctly what day Beastie had destroyed the ball.

She poured Conrad another ale and slid it over in front of him before he could finish his first one.

"I'm not done yet," he said, gesturing to his still half-full glass.

"I know," she said.

If she couldn't be ready for anything else, she could be ready for Conrad's next drink.

Roan appeared next to her, his presence grounding her. Maybe she didn't know what their future held, but if the two of them were together for it, she had no doubt that it would be okay.

Even if they forgot everything, they would find their way to each other again.

At least, she hoped that was how it would work.

She sighed and reached over to take his hand, needing a little extra comfort for a moment. Roan laced his fingers through hers and squeezed tightly. Their hands were beneath the bar, so Conrad shouldn't have been able to see anything, but he looked between the two of them in suspicion.

"You two look awful cozy," he said, directing his thoughts to Abigail, who could feel herself blushing.

"Knock it off, Conrad," Roan said.

"I'm just saying," Conrad said, raising his hands in innocence. "I like it."

"I'm sure you do," Roan said, glaring at him.

"I think I'm gonna go talk to Tanner," Conrad said with a grin, taking the full glass and leaving the bar.

Abigail let herself lean into Roan's side a little, her head resting on his shoulder.

"One more night," she said.

"I know." Roan's voice was as heavy as she felt.

"You still don't remember," she said. It wasn't a question.

"No." The words were harsh, so reminiscent of the Roan before the curse.

She hadn't missed that. "We'll figure it out," she said quietly.

Roan sighed and let go of her hand to wrap his arm around her waist and pull her closer. "I know we will, darling." He pressed a kiss to her forehead and Abigail tried not to melt into his arms.

Tomorrow, they would find out what was going to happen.

Tonight, she would savor every moment with him.

Abigail woke the next morning with a sense of finality in her bones.

It was the last day.

She'd done everything she could, and now it was up to Roan and the curse.

The sun had not yet risen, but she could tell it was coming, and she couldn't sleep anymore, so she got up and started making tea. If she couldn't sleep, at least she could get something done.

She made her way out into the tavern, planting her hands on her hips as she looked around the room at everything she had accomplished since the curse sent them back in time.

The whole room felt different with the curtains gone. Even in the early morning, with the light barely beginning to shine through, the room felt bigger and brighter, and it almost sparkled after all the cleaning she had done.

The warm glow of the dream world almost existed in the waking world as the sunrise began peeking through the windows.

She looked around in satisfaction, her eyes landing on the tapestry that Roan's grandmother had made with the lucky goat embroidered on it. She frowned at the rip, which seemed as if it had grown larger this week, though surely it hadn't.

Perhaps Roan wouldn't mind her fixing it now that things had changed between them. But perhaps it was best to ask for permission first this time, instead of throwing herself into it as she always did and getting in trouble for it.

She made her way back to the kitchen just in time as Beastie bounded in and scratched at the back door.

"Good morning, Beastie," she said, scratching under her ear as she opened the door and let her out.

She followed Beastie into the garden, sitting down on the edge of one of the beds that they'd fixed together and drawing in a few deep breaths of the fresh morning air. There was something special about an early summer morning when the breeze went through your hair. It was perfect.

Except for the lingering realization that everything could be ripped away from her after today.

She took a deep breath. She couldn't worry about that now—if she did, she would be worrying all day, and she had a few more tasks to accomplish before, if all went well, life returned to normal.

She made her way back into the kitchen, and Roan was there putting the kettle back on.

"Good morning," he said, his voice rough with sleep and his hair mussed. "You're up early."

"I couldn't sleep," she admitted. "You're putting the kettle on?"

Roan grinned. "I am capable of doing some things for myself," he said. "I know you do most of them when we're here, but believe it or not, I do actually take care of myself when I'm at home."

"I am glad to see that you have those skills," she teased, "and that you're not entirely reliant upon me."

Roan smiled but ducked his head. "I'm more reliant upon you than you know," he said.

"I know." Abigail grinned. "And don't forget it. I do have a question for you, however."

Roan glanced at her sideways.

She took a deep breath. "May I mend your grandmother's tapestry before the tear gets any worse? I realize I should have asked for permission before trying to do it last time, and I'm sorry that I didn't, but I really want to fix it so that it doesn't get worse, because I know how important the tapestry is to you and how important the tavern is. And I would hate to see something that your grandmother worked so hard on fall apart because it wasn't fixed when

I know that I can fix it, and I—hopefully you won't even be able to notice and—"

"Abigail," Roan said, cutting her off.

"I talk too much, I know," she said, wilting a little, looking down at her feet. "Sorry, I just got nervous."

"You may fix it," he said, reaching over to lift her chin so she looked at him. "And I'm sorry I was such a beast last time, when you were only trying to fix it for me. That was unkind of me, and I'm sorry."

She wrinkled her nose at him. "It was a little," she admitted. "You're sure I can fix it?"

"I trust you," he said.

Warmth flooded Abigail at those words. He trusted her. That was something she hadn't heard him say...ever. And judging by how surprised he looked, perhaps he hadn't ever said it before.

"Do you want help getting it down?" he asked.

"Yes, please," Abigail said. "I don't need to fall off the ladder again, even if you're there to catch me."

"I'll always catch you." She warmed at his words. "But still, I'd rather you didn't fall."

They could agree on that, at least.

Abigail reached for her sewing bag, and they made their way out into the tavern. Roan took the ladder from underneath the attic hatch, placing it just to the side of the tapestry.

She reached for a rung as if she was going to climb it, and Roan frowned, putting himself between her and it.

"I'll get it," he said. "No more ladders for you."

"I can manage a ladder just fine if someone doesn't scare me by shouting out my name," she pointed out. "I took down all the curtains, didn't I?"

Roan didn't say anything, simply gave her a withering glare as he began to climb the ladder. Abigail rolled her eyes—she wasn't helpless—but stood at the bottom anyway.

She wasn't sure what she was going to do if he fell. She certainly couldn't catch him the way he'd caught her, but she felt better standing near him.

She watched as he carefully unhooked the tapestry, then shifted his weight to lean toward her. The ladder shifted and her heart lurched with it. She reached out to grab it, and when she looked up at Roan, he was smirking at her.

Of course he was.

It was normal for her to be concerned for someone's safety. He didn't need to smirk like that.

"Can you take this?" he asked, leaning down with the tapestry draped over his arm.

“Of course,” she said, letting go of the ladder to take it from him.

It was heavy.

She inspected it carefully as Roan climbed down the ladder. His grandmother had clearly been an expert craftsman, and aside from the tear, it was in excellent shape.

“What caused the tear?” Abigail asked as Roan took the tapestry from her and carried it over to the bar, where she perched on a bar stool and reached for her needle and thread.

“There was a brawl,” Roan said, disgust lacing the words.

“Who started it?” Abigail asked.

“It was before you came,” he said, “and I never let the instigators come back. That was the first brawl Beastie broke up. She was so young then, and she did an incredible job. And ever since then, I let her handle any issues as they start to come up. You know everyone has a healthy fear of her now.” He grinned. “That’s why. In order to get the first instigator off the second, she grabbed his arm with her mouth to pull him away.”

Abigail grimaced at the thought of those huge jaws locking down around her arm.

"She did it gently," Roan said, his pride evident as he began wiping down the counter, though it hardly needed it. "But I'm sure you can imagine."

Abigail let out a grunt. "I wouldn't want to be him."

"Me neither," Roan said. "So you can see why he isn't coming back. Not that I would allow him to, even if he wanted to."

Abigail found the thread that matched the deep green the best before inspecting the tear once more to ascertain where she should start. She placed the needle at the edge of the tapestry and tested carefully to see if she could push it through, but the needle slipped through and pricked her finger.

"Ouch," she said, shaking her hand before bringing her finger to her mouth to suck on the prick.

"What's wrong?" Roan asked, dropping the pitcher he had been moving and hurrying to her side.

Abigail inspected her finger, watching as a tiny dot of blood welled up. "I just pricked myself. I don't think I got any blood on the tapestry."

Roan took her hand in his, inspecting it for a moment, before leaning forward and placing a gentle kiss on her knuckles. "I'm not worried about the tapestry. I care more about you."

At his words, a beam of light began to show from her finger.

Abigail's eyes widened.

Was this the end of the curse?

Chapter Thirteen
Roan

Roan stared at the beam of light coming from the blood on Abigail's finger and his eyes widened at the implication.

Was...was this really happening?

Was that it?

Had they really broken the curse after everything?

How had Abigail pricking her finger broken the curse?

There had to be something else.

He thought back to the moment the man had pointed the wand at him, and the light had poured out of it. There was no other reason for light to appear like that, and he'd said that when Roan could care for something more than he cared for his tavern...

Roan blinked. He'd told Abigail that he didn't care about the tapestry.

"We did it," he breathed. "That was the curse. I had to care about something more than my tavern. And I care about you."

Abigail's breath caught, and he looked down at her, his lips curving up into a smile.

"You were right," he said. "We did figure it out."

"I told you we would," she said, smiling up at him as he brought her hands to his chest, leaning in closer.

Her gaze dropped to his lips, and his heart beat faster as she seemed to lean closer, too.

If it wasn't Abigail, he might have simply swooped her up and kissed her in his excitement for the curse to be broken. But this wasn't any woman. This was Abigail—his Abigail—and he had no intention of scaring her away by moving too quickly.

"Roan," she said quietly, even as she moved closer, "we should—"

Footsteps sounded outside the room, and they pulled away from each other to look up as the men stumbled out of the storage room.

They looked terrible.

Roan grimaced. “Hello, gentlemen,” he said. “Had a good sleep?”

Conrad slumped over the bar as he settled on his favorite bar stool.

“I feel like I haven’t slept in a week,” he said. “What was in the ale last night? I’ve never felt like this before.”

“Let me get you sorted,” Abigail said cheerfully, hopping up and pushing the tapestry toward Roan. “I’ll be right back.”

She practically ran to the kitchen, and Roan addressed the men staring at him like they hadn’t just witnessed Abigail running away from him.

“We need to get you all some food,” Roan said. “We discovered a batch of ale had gone bad after we’d served it to you. We will be testing all of them going forward to make sure it never happens again. Your tabs have been forgiven, and Abigail is going to get you some soup right away to help settle your stomachs.”

The men grumbled to each other as they all settled into the booths and around the tables.

Roan didn’t feel like joining them. He’d been so close to kissing her before they all interrupted—and even if they didn’t realize what they’d done, he was grumpy about it.

"It was a good night, though," Tanner said, looking at everyone. "I never expected to see you dancing like that, Edgar."

Edgar grunted. "I never expected it either, but one does not say no when a young woman like Miss Abigail offers to dance with you."

The men guffawed, and Roan grinned as he headed toward the kitchen to check on Abigail, who was—as he'd expected—quickly heating up soup. Roan reached for the stack of bowls and laid out eight of them, collecting eight spoons and setting them inside before grabbing two trays.

Abigail began pouring the heated soup into the bowls, and Roan sliced the bread, anticipating her every move as he shuffled around her and put a piece of bread on top of each bowl. They worked in harmony, and not for the first time, Roan couldn't imagine a world where he didn't have Abigail working with him.

"What do you think about the time thing?" he said quietly.

"I'm expecting the man who cast it to be back this afternoon," she said. "And I assume that we're picking up where we left off, but I don't know. I've never dealt with a spell that manipulates time before."

"I didn't forget," he told her.

Abigail set the pot down and looked up at him, chewing on her bottom lip. “I didn’t either,” she said. “But I don’t know if that means there’s more coming, or if we will forget once we fall asleep, or if we’re simply not going to forget. I’ve never done this before.”

“You already said that,” he pointed out.

“It’s still true.” Her voice wobbled. “Roan, I don’t know—”

Beastie slipped into the kitchen through the swinging door and let out a yip.

Abigail sighed and looked up at him, her eyes growing misty.

“We’ll talk in a minute,” Roan said, reaching for her and pulling her into his arms for a hug.

“We need to bring them soup,” she mumbled into his chest.

“Take a deep breath first.” His gravelly voice rumbled through his chest, calming her.

Abigail obediently took a deep breath before pulling away from him and reaching for a tray. He grabbed the second and made his way out of the swinging door, holding it open for Abigail.

They were met with weak cheers, and they quickly served bowls to each of the men.

"You're a good dancer, Miss Abigail," Tanner said, the young man's eyes full of admiration.

Roan tamped down the jealousy that surged forward. Tanner was no competition, no matter what his gut tried to tell him.

"Thank you, Tanner," Abigail said, patting his shoulder in the way she would pat Beastie's head.

Roan grinned. No, Tanner was no competition.

"You know, I haven't danced like that in years," Edgar told Abigail as she served him his bowl. "You sure did take something out of me."

"I'm sorry," she said sweetly, turning the spoon so Edgar didn't have to reach for it. "I hope this will help."

Roan wasn't sure if she had enhanced the soup or not, but everyone ate it so quickly, he could see their bodies beginning to perk up again.

He was glad to see it—he felt less guilty as he watched them grow hale and hearty before his eyes again.

"I think they'll be all right," Abigail said quietly as she came up next to him behind the bar, slipping her hand into his. The way she did it automatically made Roan feel lighter.

"Hey, Abigail, another bowl!" Travis shouted.

"Excuse you," Roan growled, starting forward, but Abigail pulled back on his hand and he stayed.

"I mean—could I have more, please, Miss Abigail?" Travis asked meekly.

"I would be happy to get you more," Abigail said with a winning smile as she hurried over to collect his bowl and return to the kitchen with it.

Roan fixed Travis with a glare, and the man withered, leaning further back in his seat.

"I think perhaps we had all better watch ourselves when it comes to Miss Abigail," Conrad teased. "I think we may have had something growing right under our noses."

Roan made eye contact with all the men in the room, daring them to say something, but they didn't, and he nodded in approval.

The door opened.

All the blood in Roan's body rushed to his head, and he could hear it roaring in his ears as the man who had cursed him walked in with a grin.

"Hello," he said, sounding a little disappointed. "I see you've managed it." He looked around the room. "Oh, wonderful job."

"No thanks to you," Roan spit out.

"Ah, let's see. I think it's all thanks to me," the man said with a glint in his eye that Roan didn't like. "Without me, you never would have discovered how to love someone other than this dusty old place."

"It's not dusty," Tanner said, and Roan would have laughed if he wasn't so upset that the man was back. "It's actually quite clean."

Conrad agreed. "Much cleaner than I remember it being."

Roan tried not to laugh.

"That's beside the point," the sorcerer said. "I don't think you realize I was rooting for you all along."

"Of course you were," Roan ground out.

"I suppose I shouldn't pick one of the roses outside, though," he said with a dangerous glint in his eye.

"Don't even think about it," Roan muttered.

The man laughed. "Yes, I think my experiment was a success. How far back did you go?" he asked. "Just for curiosity's sake."

Roan didn't say anything. Everyone in the tavern was watching, and he didn't want to clue them in. The less they knew, the better. He didn't want them sniffing around Abigail and discovering her secret.

"I think you'd better leave," he said.

But then the kitchen door opened, and Abigail walked in.

Roan's heart just stopped as the sorcerer turned, his expression changing when he saw Abigail, glaring at her.

"I don't need to leave," he said, "because that's my daughter."

Chapter Fourteen
Abigail

Abigail's stomach twisted as she looked at her father.

How had he found her?

And how dare he think that she would be willing to let him stay?

And more importantly, was he the man who had cursed Roan? How had her father gotten so tangled up in time magic?

"I am no longer your daughter," she said as firmly as she could, hoping her voice would not tremble and betray her nerves. She stepped up next to Roan—perhaps standing with him would give her strength. "You lost the right to claim me when you tried to force me to marry a man who didn't want me."

He gave her a sickly-sweet smile. "Now sweetheart, you know I was only trying to provide for you."

Abigail began trembling. This is what he always did, and what she'd let him get away with for most of her life. She'd stopped letting him use her magic, but she'd never been able to stand up to the rest of his abuse.

"Abigail is under my protection, and I won't have you intimidating her, no matter what you think you're allowed to do." Roan's voice was strong and sure, even as he stared down the man who had cursed him.

If only she had that strength.

She couldn't believe this was real. How had her father gotten to the point of cursing people?

He didn't look well. His hair was unkempt, his beard looked as if he hadn't trimmed it since her would-be wedding, and there were holes in his cloak.

Holes that she would have mended for him.

"She's my daughter, and she's going to help me." Milton Lohndrey's eyes grew wild, and Roan stepped between the two of them. "She's always helped me."

She should have known that he was the man behind the curse. She hadn't known anyone else who was strong enough to cast something like this...but she never would have guessed that he'd turn to dark magic. Where was he getting the power? The dragon eggs that he pilfered were not strong enough to cast such a spell.

She poked her head around Roan's shoulder to watch as the man who'd raised her grinned at her.

Maybe she shouldn't have looked around Roan.

She reached for Roan's hand, but he flinched away from her, and Abigail suddenly felt as if she might vomit. Did he think she had something to do with this?

She'd had no idea that it was her father. Perhaps she could have guessed, but she'd had no reason to assume he'd appear after so long and curse Roan.

Did he even know she was here when he cast the spell? Probably not, or he would have been more calculated.

She sighed, pain slicing through her chest. If only she could have guessed that it was him before this had become an issue.

Before Roan assumed she was in cahoots with her father.

"Now, my precious little Abigail, you're going to help me," Milton said.

"Help you?" she scoffed. "I would sooner help anyone in the world than I would help you do anything ever again."

"You are nothing more than my pawn," her father said.

The words hit hard. She had been raised by him to believe that they were true, that she was nothing without him, that she was only there to amplify his own power.

But she had learned differently in the past year.

She had learned that she was strong enough on her own, and that she had a power inside of her that was worth more than he had ever let her believe.

She knew that now, and she would never forget it again.

"You're wrong," she said, stepping forward to stand beside Roan, whether he wanted her to or not.

At least he didn't step away from her.

"I am so much more than someone who is only meant to be your puppet. I would never dream of helping you hurt someone I care about, and I will never help you ever again. You may be my father, but I want nothing to do with you. I never wish to see you again."

Her father pulled his wand out of his pocket and pointed it at her. "You'll regret this," he said.

Roan immediately pushed her behind him, stepping forward to take the brunt of her father's wrath, but Abigail fought her way around him. He was not allowed to sacrifice himself for her.

"You taught me that the only thing I was useful for was amplifying other people," she said firmly, "but I am more than that, and I'm not going to let you destroy this home that I have built for myself and the other people here. You do not have that power."

If someone had asked her to describe how she could use her magic, she couldn't have answered. It came from inside her. Her power didn't show in a flashy ball of light like her father's, or a potion like an herbwitch's, or even come borrowed from a dragon egg.

It was a part of her, and when she wanted things to be something, they became it.

As she spoke the words, proclaiming this tavern to be her home and a safe place for all who entered it, she could feel it becoming true.

This was her magic, and it was more powerful than she could have ever imagined.

Her father turned a sickly yellow-green and stumbled back, his wand faltering as her magic made him unwelcome.

"This tavern is a safe space for all who enter it, and it will not become a place of fighting and hurt because of you. You need to leave and never come back," Abigail said steadily, "or I will let Beastie repay you for hurting Roan."

Beastie let out a fierce bark, and Abigail took special delight in watching the fear on her father's face. "She's already practically ripped someone's arm off once before," she added.

Her father's eyes widened, and he put his wand back in his pocket. "You're not worth it," he said, snarling at her. "You never have been."

He turned and fled.

Abigail was instantly surrounded by the men of the tavern as she stumbled backwards, beginning to tremble from the use of that much magic at one time.

Tanner and Conrad were the first to reach her. Tanner threw his arms around her and squeezed her tight until Conrad peeled him off. "Leave her alone, kid," he warned.

Edgar, the grumpy old coot, was exuberantly patting her on the back, and Travis and Tom offered their congratulations and thanks...but that was it.

Where was Roan?

Abigail turned to find Roan a full three paces back, his arms crossed across his chest and an unsettling look on his face.

"I didn't know," she said simply. "If I had, I would have told you."

Roan didn't say anything, so she took a step forward. "I know you have no reason to believe me. I know that you must be scared he'll come back again because of me, or he'll somehow find a way to use me against you. You must think that I'm a terrible human being because he's my father, and I promise I'm not."

Her heart was in her throat as she took another slow step. His face hadn't changed, and his eyes were studying her like he had never seen her before. "You are the best man I have ever known, Roan. You are strong and brave and kindhearted, and yes, you're a little grumpy, but I know that you would never willingly hurt me."

All the men in the tavern were watching, but she knew she had to say the rest or she'd never forgive herself. "No matter how much I want a future with you, if you can't because of my father, I will understand, and I will go, and I will never come back, because you deserve to find happiness no matter who it's with. I can only hope that the woman who steals your heart will know exactly how lucky she is."

She closed the last step between them and looked up at Roan, her eyes pleading for him to understand. "I love you, Roan. So whatever is going through your head right now, I desperately hope that it has something to do with the fact that you love me, too."

"Have I ever told you before that you talk too much?" Roan asked, the corner of his mouth turning up into a smile as he leaned down and cupped her cheek with his hand before pressing his lips to hers.

The tavern erupted into cheers, and Abigail sighed with relief as she returned his kiss, throwing her arms around his neck and holding him tight.

"You might have mentioned it once or twice," she said, fighting back tears. Beastie, sensing a celebration, jumped up on the two of them, resting her large paws on Roan's arm.

"Beastie knows," Roan said. "I love you, too, and I hope the three of us can be together for the rest of our lives."

"I would love nothing more," she whispered, dangerously close to tears as Roan shook Beastie off.

"I'm sorry that I doubted you for even a moment." He wrapped an arm around her waist and pulled her closer, using his other hand to tuck her hair behind her ear. "I should have known you would never be part of that. Especially after what you told me about your childhood, I should have known better. For him to claim you as his daughter when he appeared surprised me so much that I couldn't think straight."

"But you still stepped between us," Abigail pointed out, resting her hand on his chest and smiling up at him.

"I would have, too," Tanner shouted before several voices told him to hush.

Abigail laughed and rested her head on Roan's chest, hoping to hide her blush from the men in the tavern. "I don't suppose you want to take this to your office?" she asked quietly.

"That sounds like a grand idea," Roan said, and she didn't have to look up to see the glare he was directing at the men. "Conrad's in charge."

He leaned down and scooped her up in his arms to a cacophony of cheers. Abigail laughed, sure that her face was as pink as his grandmother's dress as he kicked the door open and walked down the hallway to his office.

"You didn't have to carry me," she teased.

"I wanted to," he said as he nudged the door shut behind them and set her down, backing her up against it.

Any other man, and she would have been intimidated. Even a week ago, this would have been too much, but now she felt nothing but happiness as he leaned against the doorway on one forearm and ran his fingers through her hair.

She felt safe.

"You saved me," he said. "If you hadn't been here, I never would have found someone that I could care for more than a tavern. None of those idiots in there would have been enough."

Abigail snorted. "You mean you wouldn't have fallen in love with Tanner?"

Roan rolled his eyes. "Tanner needs to grow up," he muttered. "The boy is going to drive me to insanity if he doesn't."

"I don't suppose anyone else would have helped you clean the tavern," Abigail said, pretending to think hard.

"As if that's the only reason I fell in love with you," Roan muttered.

Her eyes filled with tears again. "You love me."

Roan smiled as he leaned down. "I do. I love you very much. And I intend to spend the rest of our lives making sure you don't forget it."

He leaned down, and she pressed up on her tiptoes to kiss him once again, and the whole world disappeared until it was just the two of them.

Was this really happening?

"You know what?" she asked.

Roan raised an eyebrow.

"I think my father cursing you might be the best thing that ever happened to me."

Ron let out a harsh laugh. "If you had told me that a week ago, I would have laughed at you."

"You just did," she pointed out.

"I would have laughed more," he said.

"Because you love to laugh so much," she teased.

He snorted, which made her laugh, which made him laugh.

Somehow they ended up sitting on the floor, leaning up against the door to his office, laughing hysterically. His arm was around her, and she leaned against him, and while she wasn't quite sure how they'd gotten here, she couldn't imagine wanting to be anywhere else.

"I am so glad it wasn't just a dream," Roan said after a moment, "even if in the beginning I thought it was a beastly dream."

"You're the only beast here," Abigail responded, enjoying the frown that creased between his eyes, because it gave her the opportunity to reach up and smooth it away. "But you're my beast."

She smiled winningly and Roan shook his head. "I suppose I can live with that," he said, leaning in to kiss her again.

Chapter Fifteen
Roan

He missed Abigail.

The thought was irritating. He had gone from being a perfectly self-sufficient man a week ago to feeling alone without her.

Roan hurried to the tavern. Maybe she would be there early.

He'd walked her home the night before—their first official outing as a couple. And today was their first day opening the tavern together since everything had happened...and it was also the day he was hoping to apologize to his brother and return the letters.

But first, he needed to see Abigail.

Beastie trotted after him as he hurried toward the tavern. Would Abigail feel the same way and also be there early, or was she enjoying the feeling of a real bed again?

He arrived at the tavern and unlocked the front door, turning to look for her before he entered the building. There she was, just coming into view, wearing a different dress than she'd been wearing, and smiling wide when she saw him.

She was perfect.

"Hello, my love," she called as she came within speaking distance.

"Hello, darling," he said, wrapping his arm around her waist the moment he could and pulling her to him.

"Did you sleep well? I missed dreaming with you," she admitted, resting her hand on his chest and smiling up at him.

He'd missed it, too. After spending nearly every moment together for the past week, it was disturbing to be alone again.

"Did you change your mind at all?" he asked. Distance might have made a difference for her, even though he hoped desperately that it didn't.

"I did not," she assured him, smiling up at him as she leaned up on her tiptoes.

He leaned down to kiss her, holding her tight in an effort to show just how much he'd missed her overnight.

If this was how they felt after one night, what was it going to be like when they spent weeks apart?

"I missed knowing you were in the same building while I was sleeping," Abigail admitted quietly. "I feel safer with you."

Roan nodded. "I felt the same way," he said. "My brother wasn't home last night—he probably slept at the orphanage—and it was odd being alone with Beastie."

He sighed and followed her into the kitchen, where she put on the kettle and he began pulling out bowls.

"Did you not eat this morning?" she asked, glancing at the bowls with a smile.

"No," he said, turning red. "I was in too much of a hurry to come see you."

Abigail laughed. "I didn't eat, either," she admitted, "for the same reason."

"This is ridiculous." Roan dropped the bowls on the counter and crossed his arms. "How are we supposed to carry on like this? We should just get married, and then I don't have to pay you, and we can just live together."

Abigail dropped the kettle and looked up at him with wide eyes.

"I mean, I wasn't really proposing," he stammered, glancing between the kettle, which had splashed water everywhere, and Abigail, "but I do think that maybe someday we should get married. I mean, if you want. Not that you have to. I know that you probably have better options. And why would you want to marry me when I'm just the tavern grump who's rude to everyone, makes mistakes, and doesn't know what he's doing? And I am sure you have better options and shouldn't waste yourself on me."

"Now who's talking too much?" Abigail teased, stepping closer and using her fingers to cover his mouth. "I don't have any better options, and we can discuss this more later. I think it's too soon, but I am definitely interested," she said with a smile, removing her fingers and pressing a quick kiss to his lips before she whirled away to grab the kettle.

"Not so fast," Roan growled, grabbing her arm and twirling her back toward him. "Do you mean that?" he asked.

Abigail's eyes softened. "I do," she said quietly. "I would love nothing more...but I do think it's too soon."

Roan sighed. "I think you're right," he said, even if he didn't like it. Beastie pushed her way in between the two of them and sat at their feet, looking up at them with her tongue out and panting.

"You just can't stand not being in the middle of things, can you?" Roan asked, reaching over to pet her at the same time Abigail did. Their fingers brushed, and Roan used the opportunity to snag her hand and slide his fingers through hers.

"I can't wait until you decide it's time," he said, squeezing her hand. "But I will wait as long as it takes."

"I will let you know," Abigail promised, pressing up on her toes to seal that promise with a kiss.

A few weeks after the curse had been broken, the tavern was completely different. Roan surveyed the room, which was full of people, and looked down at Abigail with a smile. She had planned this event to celebrate his birthday, but the real present was her. She was wearing his grandmother's gown, looking absolutely stunning, and he had never been happier.

Everyone was here—his brother Nathaniel and his sweetheart, all their regulars, the blacksmith and his daughter, and more, including guests he didn't quite recognize by name but recognized anyway.

It was an event fit for a king. Not that he was the king, but he felt like it as he looked around the room full of people, all of whom were paying him for food and drink, and the woman he loved. She had taken the budget from running negative every month to having extra this month, and this party promised to add even more to their coffers.

Which was perfect, because he wanted to propose to Abigail, and he needed to buy a ring.

Abigail brought out a whole mess of pies she had been baking all day, and Conrad reached over and helped himself to a piece promptly.

"I wasn't serving that yet," Abigail said with a teasing tone before walking away.

"She shouldn't have put it in front of me, then," Conrad pointed out, but he wasn't talking to Roan. He was watching a young woman with coppery hair and a bright smile who was talking to Nathaniel and Thea.

"Who is she?" Roan asked, bumping Conrad on the shoulder.

"Her name is Linnea," Conrad responded. "She's training to cover the café while Nathaniel and Thea go on their honeymoon."

Roan glanced at Linnea in surprise. He wouldn't have picked her to be Conrad's type, but Conrad hadn't stopped looking at her since she entered the room. "Go for it, man," he told him. "Women may be difficult sometimes, but they're worth it."

"I heard that," Abigail said, appearing next to him with a mischievous grin. "I'm difficult?"

"In the best way possible, darling," Roan said, pulling her close and wrapping his arm around her waist. "May I have this dance?"

"You're just trying to get me to forget that you called me difficult," she said, a wicked smile on her face, but she took the hand he held out and allowed him to lead her to the dance floor.

Well, it wasn't quite a dance floor, but a bit of extra space in the middle of the tavern counted.

At Roan's nod, Lyle picked up his fiddle and began to play a merry tune. Abigail looked up at him, a question in her eyes, and Roan twirled her instead of answering. Yes, he'd arranged it with Lyle. Dancing with Abigail was one of his favorite things to do. "I love you," he said, after twirling her and dipping her down before pulling her back up. "Thank you for fixing everything."

"It's what I do," Abigail said, her eyes twinkling. "I improve everything."

"Well, you've certainly improved me," Roan said.

As they twirled around the floor, other couples joining them, satisfaction pulsed through him.

She had improved more than just him—she'd impacted everyone in this tavern for the better.

He couldn't wait to see what else they would improve, together, for the rest of their lives.

EPILOGUE

ABIGAIL AND ROAN ENTERED the Cozy Cat Café hand in hand.

Roan's brother Nathaniel and his wife Thea had been married for several months, and they were finally going on their honeymoon. They were here to say goodbye...and to make sure Linnea knew that they were here if she needed help.

Though Abigail wouldn't be surprised if Conrad also volunteered his assistance.

"Aren't you glad you brought their letters back?" Abigail whispered as they waited in line to purchase something. She firmly believed in supporting other businesses, especially when they were owned by family.

Roan simply gave her a look, and Abigail resisted the urge to giggle.

Nat and Thea were an absolutely adorable couple, and she loved watching them work together on the other side of the counter. They hadn't noticed Abigail and Roan in the line yet, and watching them work together in perfect harmony was always so enjoyable. And fortunately, they didn't hate Roan for stealing their letters—at least, they said they didn't.

Abigail and Thea had become fast friends, and the brothers were working on their relationship. Things were going well, at least as far as Abigail was concerned.

"I can't believe they're actually going on a honeymoon," Abigail said, reaching for Roan's hand simply because she could.

"I can," Roan said. "It's just the sort of thing he always wanted to do—go back to Riyel. It doesn't surprise me at all that he wants to take her back there now that they're married, so they can see it all one more time. I can't believe they're leaving the café, though."

"Would you ever leave the tavern?" Abigail asked.

Roan looked down at her with such alarm written on his face that she couldn't help giggling.

"I'm not saying we should," she said. "I'm asking if you would."

"If you wanted me to," Roan said slowly, but the words were shaky, and she wasn't sure she believed him.

"I'm not asking," she added, patting his arm so he could take a breath again.

Ron sighed dramatically. "Oh, good. I don't think there's anyone I would trust with it—yet."

"Maybe Morgan," Abigail said, referring to the blacksmith's daughter who occasionally helped her. "But no, you're right. I can't think of anyone else."

Nathaniel caught sight of them and offered a brief nod. His hand reached out to snag Thea's elbow, and he pointed her attention to them.

Thea smiled and hurried out to give Abigail a hug, while Nathaniel and Roan clasped hands over the counter.

It was better than nothing.

"I can't believe you're actually leaving," Abigail said.

"I know," Thea said, anxious excitement in her voice.

"I'm so nervous," Linnea admitted from the other side of the counter.

"But I know you'll be here to help if she needs it," Thea said.

"Of course we will," Abigail said, looking up at Roan with a smile. "The café tends to be busier before we are, so I'll pop in to check on her and make sure she doesn't need anything. Roan can manage the tavern on his own if things get busy here."

"That's what you think," Roan said.

Abigail patted his arm. "You'll be fine, dear. I'm looking forward to spending a little more time with Linnea." And not just because Conrad had started acting a little shy anytime the café was mentioned, but because she seemed lovely. "It will be great and you will have a wonderful trip. I know it."

Nathaniel came around the counter and reached for his wife's hand. "The cart is loaded," he said, smiling down at her. "Are you ready to go?"

"I just have to say goodbye to Ginger first," she added, hurrying over to the fireplace where the café's namesake, a long-haired orange cat, was sitting and waiting for them. She said goodbye to the cat, and then Nat and Thea left, leaving Abigail and Roan with a very nervous Linnea standing behind the counter.

Abigail let a bit of her magic slip out to ease the poor girl's nerves, improve the peace in the building, and make everything taste a little bit better.

"Everything will be fine," she told Linnea. "You'll see."

"Thank you," the girl said with a shaky smile. "I hope I'll do them proud."

"I'm sure you will," Abigail said before reaching for Roan's hand. "We'll be down at the tavern, but I'll come and check on you if you need me."

"Thank you," Linnea said, sounding only slightly terrified as they left the café.

Abigail let Roan pull her back toward the tavern. It was faster than she would have liked to walk, but he always got antsy when he was away from the Lucky Goat.

"I thought we'd never get back," he teased as he unlocked the building.

"Oh, was there something you desperately needed to do?" she quipped.

"Yes," he said, twirling her into his arms like they were dancing and dipping her backward to kiss her dramatically before pulling her back up into his chest.

Abigail flushed. "That was a good reason, I suppose," she said, resting her hand on his chest. "I love you."

"I love you, too," he said, pressing a kiss to her forehead as Beastie came bounding out of the kitchen toward them. He'd installed a door for her so she could go out in the backyard whenever she wanted, and she was much happier now.

So was Abigail.

She had never been more joyful, and as she let a little magic seep out into the room around them, she knew it would only get better from here.

***

See Roan propose to Abigail in their bonus epilogue at https://chickadeelanepress.com/beastly-epilogue

Not ready to leave Galamere yet?

- See Nathaniel and Thea's side of things in Once Upon A Cat.
- Read Conrad and Linnea's romance in A Taste of Tea and Tenderness.
- Or start the series with Nathaniel and Thea's first chance romance, Tales of Cake and Comfort.

Thank you so much for reading Beastly Dreams! If you enjoyed it, would you mind leaving a review? Reviews help indie authors more than you know!

And if you want to learn more about my upcoming work, you can join my newsletter at

https://chickadeelanepress.com/newsletter.

Hardcover Epilogue

"Introducing Mr. and Mrs. Roan and Abigail Alder!" Conrad shouted, bringing loud cheers and the sound of glasses clinking and feet stomping.

"If they break any of those glasses, they're in trouble," Roan muttered as he and Abigail ran through the doorway into the tavern.

Before they could get far, a bouquet of flowers smacked him in the face.

"What was that?" he growled.

"You're supposed to throw them one at a time." Conrad said to Tanner, smacking him upside the head, "not the whole thing."

"You didn't tell me that part!" Tanner protested as he moved towards them.

"Congratulations!" Edgar said, hobbling up to Abigail and giving her a hug. "I always knew you could tame the beast."

"She didn't tame anything," Roan growled. "Get your hands off my wife, Tanner."

"I was just saying congratulations," Tanner said, backing away from Abigail with his hands in the air.

Roan didn't believe him.

"He was, dear," Abigail said, patting Roan on the arm as more well-wishers gathered around them.

Roan looked around the Lucky Goat, full of people and full of love, and smiled—even if only inwardly.

It wouldn't do to let everyone here know just how much he'd fallen head over heels. As far as they were concerned, he was still the grumpy old tavern owner, and if anyone in this tavern ever dared to disrespect his wife, they would have him to deal with.

What had changed was how ferociously they would be dealt with.

Roan glowered as all the men came up to congratulate his wife, and very few of them said anything to him.

"You're going to scare them all away," Conrad pointed out.

"That's the point," Roan said, as a relatively new patron hugged Abigail a little too long. "We're going behind the bar."

"You don't have to be so protective, dear," Abigail said with a laugh, patting his arm.

"Yeah, you don't have to be so protective, dear," Conrad said with a grin.

Roan elbowed Conrad, making him wobble on his barstool. "Don't make me eject you."

"All right, all right. Settle down, everyone!" Conrad yelled.

Roan rolled his eyes. When had Conrad decided that he was second in command here?

He supposed it wasn't the worst thing, though. It did mean that he could sneak away with his wife if he wanted to, and right now he wanted to sneak into the kitchen and kiss her senseless.

"We'll be right back," he told Conrad, who gave him an amused grin.

As Roan pulled his wife back into the kitchen, Beastie followed closely behind.

"I'm fine," Abigail said, letting out a sigh as she looked up at him while he pulled her close. "You don't need to be so protective."

"And that's where you're mistaken, darling," he said, tucking a loose strand of hair behind her ear. "I'll protect you for the rest of my life, and you're just going to have to get used to it."

Abigail smiled. "I suppose I did sign up for that when I married you."

"You knew I was a beast before you married me, and wild animals do tend to be territorial," he pointed out.

Abigail reached up to cup his cheek with her tiny hand. "I love you," she said. "Even if you are overly territorial."

"There's no such thing," Roan said, leaning down to kiss his wife.

Beastie yipped, and he looked down at his faithful friend and shook his head. "You're just going to have to get used to this, Beastie. You're going to see a lot more of it."

"Is that so?" his wife murmured.

Roan pulled her close, leaning down once again.

"Absolutely."

AUTHOR NOTE

I HOPE YOU LOVED Abigail and Roan as much as I do! I'll be honest, I wasn't sure Roan could be redeemed...but then Abigail appeared in my head and wouldn't go away!

(And if you're wondering more about her father, the two of them make an appearance in Once Upon A Rose, when her father tried to marry her off to Lord Dunham.)

You can learn more about upcoming books in the world of Galamere by joining my newsletter at chickad eelanepress.com/newsletter, or following me online—I'm @LandiWrites in most places! I'd love to meet you around the internet!

Wishing you fluffy blankets, warm drinks, and cozy books,

Gabrielle

READY FOR CONRAD'S STORY?

A TASTE OF TEA AND TENDERNESS

READY FOR
NAT AND THEA'S STORY?

ONCE
UPON A
CAT

Acknowledgements

To all my Displaced ladies—thank you for letting me join you for this amazing series!!

This book would not be nearly as good without the help of my beta readers, editor, and friends I've bounced ideas off of. Abby, Anabelle, Coral, Eliza, Kat, Lisa—thank you!!

Thank you to all of my readers, those who have championed this new series, and to anyone who I accidentally forgot to mention by name. LOL

And finally, a huge thank you to my family. Your support keeps me going and I love you all so very much! <3

About the Author

Gabrielle Landi lives in Southern Indiana with her husband and children and has a soft spot for every stray cat that ends up on her front porch. When she's not writing, she spends her time chasing children, wishing there was more coffee, and eating chocolate like it's her job. If she had to write her own love story in tropes, it would include second chance romance and a secret relationship, and would be entirely unbelievable.

Follow online at:

ChickadeeLanePress.com

Facebook: Author Gabrielle Landi

Instagram: @LandiWrites

TikTok: @LandiWrites